ONE VOW

FRAT HOUSE SCANDAL
BOOK TWO

SUMMER COOPER

LOVY BOOKS

1

Finn

The emergency room at Aspen Memorial Hospital was packed. The smell of blood was as potent as the antiseptic cleansers we used to clean the floor.

Doctors shouted orders.

Machines whirred and beeped.

Lives hung in the balance.

One patient after another rolled through the glass doors on gurneys or staggered through to collapse when they should've been on a gurney as rain pounded the windows. The rain was probably more than 40 percent responsible for such a busy night. The problem was, I couldn't concentrate on of any the patients because I had one angry fiancée threatening all that I hold dear. Which was hardly surprising since that was how she'd managed to become my fiancée in the first place.

A nurse passed. "Dr. Makenzie, can you help with bed two?"

I held up one finger. Dr. Finn Makenzie, me, needed to see patients, not be embroiled in what had the potential to be the drama of the century. Yet I stayed in the cubicle with my fiancée because there was no telling how she would punish me for whatever I'd done to piss her off now.

I yanked the blue curtain closed as if it might muffle the sounds about to erupt from the mouth of the ever-so-steely Beth Cooper, not the sounds that raged around us. Beth stood in front of me with her cheeks flushed red under her makeup and her eyes narrowed so that all I could see were lashes and anger.

"What the hell are you talking about, Beth?" Beth and I had gone to the prestigious Glouster University together once upon a time, and somehow, ten years after graduation, she managed to track me down and blackmail me into marriage.

There were at least ten people who needed me more than she did out there, but Beth didn't care about that, all she cared about was herself. Lacerations. Broken bones. A case of dehydration and a migraine. And whatever the hell was going on in bed two needed me to be the doctor that I was, but Beth came first.

In the grand scheme of things, a wedding I didn't want to happen that now wouldn't happen didn't measure up to what the patients were going through. Truth be told, I didn't care about said wedding. Not that it mattered to Beth. She was fierce and angry, panicked to the point of mania. In other words, a normal day for her.

"I said the reason they wouldn't give us the license this morning is because you're still married." She wasn't quite shrieking yet, but history, along with the vein throbbing in her forehead said it wouldn't be long.

Beth Cooper was the definition of high-maintenance: weekly manicure, monthly hair appointments with Renaldo to maintain her Marilyn Monroe Platinum hair, an annual clothing budget that could purchase a nice three-bedroom in Glouster, and Botox injections from Dr. Capaldi, plastic surgeon to the stars.

"Well, that can't be right. I signed the papers over a decade ago." Whatever clerical genius messed this up was getting a bottle of 80-year-old whiskey from my Christmas gift list.

"Did you send them back?" She had one hip cocked and a hand clutched onto it.

"Of course, I sent them back." I checked my watch because this conversation had gone on about three minutes longer than it should have. And the look on her face, irate red cheeks; enraged flashing eyes, and a ready-to-kill sneer, meant that unless I found a way to stop it, it wasn't going to be ending any time soon. "Look, Beth, I have patients to see. Can we possibly talk about this later?"

"No. No. No! We can't talk about this later!" And now she was shrieking. "You're married to someone else! And we're supposed to be walking down the aisle in nine days. Nine!"

She closed her eyes and breathed out slowly. I'd seen her do this before. About a hundred times already. And there was nothing I could do to stop the snowball effect of bad behavior. The cursing. The screaming. The tears. And I was powerless to stop it. "And you're married to someone else. Do you know what that means?"

It meant we weren't going to be able to get married. No Cooper/Makenzie wedding at the Beverly Hills Hotel. Had she not been standing in front of me with her green eyes flashing fire and her fists clenching like the only thing keeping her from punching me was the three feet of space between us, I might have done the happy dance, or the thrilled beyond comprehension tango, or the yay I didn't have to marry the wicked witch shuffle. But she started moving closer, and it wasn't like I could back up.

"Okay, so we have to postpone." Her eyes widened and her breath came in short angry huffs. "Look, it's only a couple months. Just let me talk to Felicity, and I'll get it straightened out."

Not that big of a deal. A few hundred phone calls. A few lost deposits we could both afford. This was nothing more than a scheduling issue. Definitely not something worthy of the tantrum. But Beth Cooper, despite her public, always smiling persona had never met a tantrum she didn't like.

"I *need* to be married. They aren't giving *my* show to Zach Wembley because of his happy wife, happy life thing. *Married people are trustworthy.*" She hissed the words in a tone too sharp and too angry for anyone's good. Especially mine. "I need the ratings our wedding will generate. I need this marriage. "And they're deciding right after Christmas. We *can't* wait a couple months."

She crossed her arms and shook her head, hair sprayed so stiff it didn't so much as shimmy. "I *won't* wait."

When I didn't move, she shoved the bed in our little cubicle toward me, then her face fell, and her eyes brimmed with tears. "This show, the audience I've built over the years, it's all I ever wanted. And I'm not going to lose out because you didn't use correct postage. Fix this!"

I sighed because what else could I do? Nothing but a trot down the aisle was going to shut her up and keep my reputation intact. No one wanted a pervert as their doctor. And she had the powerful medium and the video to spin the story she was threatening to tell. Shit.

"What do you expect me to do, Beth? How the hell am I supposed to find someone to cover my shifts, hunt down Felicity, and get divorced in nine days?" That damned video had cost me enough already. I wasn't going to sacrifice the reputation I'd worked so hard to build and then protect. So, by God, if marrying Beth Cooper was the only way to keep it quiet, then I'd marry her.

Her voice was smaller, less frantic than just a second ago. "I want you to fly to Maine and talk to the crazy she-bat. You tell her if she doesn't want her sex video, which makes her look like some penis-crazy nympho, to go public, she'll divorce you right now."

"I don't even know if she still lives in Maine."

"Of course, she does. She's too pathetic to go anywhere else." She yanked a folded piece of paper from her pocket. "She even lives in the same freaking house. And you need to go talk to her. Use that Makenzie charm and get her to divorce you."

She stamped her foot, a petulant move in my book, but it was Beth, so it wasn't beyond her. "Right now! Because so help me God, if I don't get this promotion, I'm taking you and her and everyone involved with these videos down. And it's a #MeToo world, Finn. You know what'll happen. Do you hear me?"

Pardon me if I wasn't exactly cartwheeling my way to the church to be married to this one. "I hear you."

Half the damned hospital heard her.

She leaned in close enough that I got a nose full of her perfume. It reminded me of crazy with a smidgeon of bitchy afternotes. My future was that smell, and I almost groaned in misery out loud, but snapped my mouth shut to hold it back.

"Make this happen, Finn." She turned and walked to the door, and I stared because there was nothing else I could do. "I'll book you a flight."

Not only would she book my flight, I wouldn't even have to worry about packing, arranging a ride to the airport, or telling whoever needed to know I would be gone for a couple days. When something mattered to Beth Cooper, it *really* mattered to Beth Cooper. And she would do whatever it took to make sure I was divorced by a week from Saturday because that was the kind of thing she did.

But what she didn't do was love anyone other than herself. And as much as I wanted to save everything I'd worked for, I couldn't imagine spending the rest of my life, or even one minute of it, tied to someone so angry and so vicious. Not when I knew what it was like to be married to a woman I loved with all my heart. But I also knew I didn't have a choice.

One Decade Ago

FROM THE MOMENT I discovered football, Sunday was always my favorite day. That came to have even more meaning when I started to play for the university's football team. Sunday was the day after the game, when we were all still heroes even if we lost. A day when we didn't have classes and could just relax. We'd watch NFL games all day long with beers and bets on the side.

This particular Sunday was wasted on me because I felt as if I had a hangover, my knee was in a splint, and my bedroom was dark. This Sunday, I wasn't a hero. I was a casualty. Tackled on fourth and goal at the one-yard line, leg bent awkward, pinned under a guy from Oklahoma who weighed in at a proud 220, all of which landed on my right leg. Hence the druggy hangover, splint, and darkness.

Monday wasn't much better, but by Tuesday I was fed up with Vicodin and decided not to watch the live stream of my classes today, a luxury afforded to athletes and distance learners. Today, I was going to grace my teachers with my presence. On crutches. I limped across the campus from the Alpha Alpha Phi fraternity house where I lived. Not my finest hour. And the next one was worse. I hobbled into class, drenched in sweat, arms aching, knee throbbing, head ready to explode.

All this effort for Anatomy and Physiology. For a class

that I could have probably passed in my sleep thanks to a photographic memory and a two-hour-a-day pre-party study time schedule, because Alpha Alpha Phi was a party frat and we partied every night.

I took the first empty seat I found and sat down. I propped my crutches on the wall beside me and wished that before I set off on my hour-long trek to class, I'd remembered my backpack with my notebook and pens.

Optimistic me thought listening might work, but the me who knew my devil that didn't give a fuck attitude was fully aware that listening without reading would never work for me. Of course, I could always just sit here for an hour and wish I wasn't thinking about my notebook and pen because a photographic memory only worked on things I could see, not what I'd heard.

The room was huge with raised seating and long curved tables broken into three sections and divided by steps leading to each tier. In front, there was a single desk and a whiteboard that ran the length of the wall. Nothing about this room was extraordinary. Nothing memorable. It was a classroom like a hundred others on campus. But it was magical. And it started with…

"Hey." The voice. Then the smile. Then the eyes. She didn't appeal to me all at once, but in waves. And it started with her voice.

"Hi," I answered while I studied her.

She wrangled her bag over my head, well, almost over except the corner that caught me in the temple.

"Sorry." She slid into the seat next to me. From the thousand pound bag that whacked me in the head, she pulled a legal pad, three pens, two high lighters, an anatomy book that accounted for the girth and weight of her bag, a twin to the one I'd left at home, and a tape recorder she set on the corner of her desk.

When she turned and flashed me another smile, I almost fell out of the chair. It was a holy shit moment, the kind a guy like me would never be lucky enough to have twice. The kind that imprinted on my guts. God, she was extraordinary in ways I didn't usually find women to be.

"No problem." And I sounded like I'd just rounded the corner from junior high to puberty. A crack that made *prob* and *lem* sound as if two different people, one an adult male and the other much younger, on the cusp of chest hair and pubes, said it.

She stared at me for a second, and my fool heart fell for her, right then. For her eyes. Blue like a summer sky. Big enough I could see, if not forever, a very long time. I fell hard enough I wasn't even bothered by the floweriness of my thoughts.

"If you hear me actually burst into tears during class, don't worry. I suck at science." She said, and her voice was music to ears that finally knew what real music was.

One more smile out of her and I was probably going to end up making a fool of myself. She was that kind of dangerous to my well-being and my cool-guy reputation. The long dark hair that curtained her face as she settled in drew my gaze and I wondered if the dark brown strands were as silky as they looked.

Before I could answer, Dr. Klein walked in, white lab coat, ruler-straight spine, wiry gray hair that sprouted from her head in about seventy directions. If she wasn't Albert Einstein's time-traveling twin, she was definitely his modern-day doppelganger. She even had the mustache.

The wonder girl next to me leaned over.

"I'm Felicity, by the way." She held out her hand. "Felicity Fields."

"Chancellor Fields' daughter?" I asked, my voice a croak again.

She nodded. And if her smile was potent, her skin was silk. Satin. Perfect. Extraordinary. "I'm…um, I'm Finn."

She chuckled. "I know who you are. We *all* know who you are."

Between the fact that the melody of her laugh had me mesmerized and that she hadn't let go of my hand yet, I could barely draw in a useful breath. And she knew who I was. That made her even hotter. Not that I would've believed it possible until I saw it with my own eyes.

Suddenly, I didn't care one damned bit about the anatomy of the musculoskeletal system. I cared about getting to know Felicity. I wanted to know what music she liked, her favorite books and classes and TV shows. I wanted to know about her family and friends. Her…everything. And it couldn't happen fast enough.

I leaned closer and caught a whiff of her. Jasmine. Lavender. And I stuttered because every word I'd ever heard or learned to say disappeared from my mind. I didn't have a single thought left. Nothing. And now I was the creepy guy in class who was sniffing the girl sitting next to him. I jerked straight and cleared my throat. Loudly. It was more a growl than a simple clear.

Dr. Klein looked at me. Of the 50 or so students in the class, she stared at me. Long. Hard. A glare, really. That glare would have shrunk a lesser man. But I was in my own world, ego charged because the pretty girl next to me knew who I was.

"All right, people. Everybody needs a partner because things are about to get very interesting."

"It's not Bio or Chem, and we aren't doing labs in this class, so what the hell do we need a partner for?" I said softly.

Yeah. It could have easily been called grumbling maybe even whining, but only because if I chose a partner, that meant I would have to come to class every Tuesday and Thursday or it wouldn't be fair to said partner. And no way in hell did I plan to come to class every Tuesday and Thursday.

But when I looked over at Felicity, she had the most adorable, pleading, wide-eyed puppy dog look on her face. And if those batting eyelashes weren't meant for me, the rest of my life was meaningless.

As soon as I had the thought, I wanted to kick my own ass. I wasn't some drama queen who needed the meaning of life. But I wanted this girl. Maybe for more than just the usual wham, bam, thank you, Finn.

I felt connected to her. Or maybe I kept my mouth shut because I was depressed and tired and horny. Plus, still hungover from the drugs. Either way, I nodded instead of explaining that the chances of me ever coming back to the live version of this class were slim.

And if my head hadn't betrayed me, my mouth was all set to give up. "Okay."

An answer I could only chalk up to letting my dick be in charge of my response.

"All right." And it took a whole minute for a grin to spread across her face and for her to lean in and whisper, "I can't wait to tell all my friends that Finn Makenzie and I are learning anatomy together."

I chuckled at the slight high school cheerleader shoulder shrug and the wiggle to her eyebrows. There was something so adorable about her.

I'd dated plenty of girls since high school. Plenty. But I'd never been so immediately in lust and hoping for more. So ready to follow her anywhere. And I hated myself for admitting it. Really hated myself.

Dr. Klein moved to the whiteboard while her assistant handed out three-inch binders full of course material. Notes. All the information that would be on the exam, sorted and organized into categories for "purposeful studying." With my partner and her beautiful blue eyes and smile that was brighter than the sun.

2

Felicity

Over the last decade, I hadn't spent much time thinking about Finn Makenzie.

Shit. That was a lie.

I spent *a lot* of time thinking of his stony gray eyes, his bright smile, and oh, the kissing. Hundreds upon hundreds of hours thinking of kissing his soft lips. The skills he had with that magical mouth of his and the way his tongue caressed and teased. Every once in a while, I remembered his touch. The friction as his fingers slid on me, or the way we used to slide together, skin against skin. Usually, I thought of him after a couple of tequila shooters or immediately preceding a long, cold shower or two.

A lot of hours.

And *that* was the truth, but never once did I imagine him knocking on my door, wearing an easy half-smile and a coat not nearly warm enough for a Maine December. But there he was, standing on my porch, same cocky smirk, same honey-gold hair, same fuck-me body.

I'd opened the door because he came back. "Hi, Lis."

I slammed it shut because it took him ten years to do it.

"Come on. Let me in, Felicity."

Oh, did I mention the voice? That low timbre, the quiet resonance that made my heart palpitate and my panties all but catch fire? Even ten years later. Although, no way in hell was I sharing that piece of information with him.

I opened the door because I was weak, but I kept my voice strong because…pride. "What do you want, Finn?"

"We need to talk."

No. Ten years ago, we needed to talk. Ten years ago, we had something to talk about. Now, we didn't. I shut the door again.

He chuckled from the other side. "Lis, we can do this all day. I'll knock. You'll open the door. I'll say something stupid, and you'll slam it shut again."

He paused just long enough for me to swallow my heart.

"But we both know every time I knock, you're going to open that door." I hated the way his voice made my heart race, even now.

"We know no such thing." I spit the words out, hissed them even. Time had healed me, cured me of my Finn addiction. But after a minute I folded, and because he was outside and I was inside and I couldn't see him, I could ask. "How do we know?"

"Because we're us."

Cured might have been a bit much to hope for. And

because no one needed proof of that more than I did, I opened the door again. "What do you want?"

He moved around me then turned to provide me the full-on Finn effect. The bedroom eyes, tongue peeking out between full, extremely kissable lips, body as perfect as I remembered, maybe better than I remembered, broad at his shoulders, tapered at his waist, with long legs and an ass I could've bounced quarters off of. If that was a thing. Which of course, it wasn't. But I was willing to give it a try.

"You look good, Lis." I'd spent the morning lugging boxes down from the attic. The red bandana holding my hair back was soaked with sweat. My hoodie was a left-over of his, and he hadn't been around in ten years of washing and drying. My jeans and probably my face had more streaks of dust than my feather duster had ever rid from my house. I aspired to good.

"You still lie like a champ, Finn." And I hated him for it. And loved him for it. And hated myself for loving him for it. Mixed emotions were tough.

He cleared his throat and smiled as he looked around. I could feel it, the way his gaze judged everything in my home. I hadn't taken down the picture of us at the beach, the sunrise over the ocean from that same morning, and the shadow box of memories I'd kept was still there because I was stronger than that damned box of movie tickets and photos and piece of shirt he'd worn to our wedding. And by God, the only reason I kept it in my sight line was to remind myself I was over him. Usually, I didn't need much reminding. Well, not as much as right then. In my defense, he was usually three thousand miles across the country.

"I would've thought you'd moved by now."

Could've. Would've. Should've. *Really* should've since I was about ten seconds from embarrassing myself by blurting out how much I missed my husband. Him. The same man who hadn't waited two full weeks before he left me.

"And leave our love nest and all those memories from our *eleven days of marriage*?" I scoffed. On the outside, unaffected. Borderline rude, even. But inside... so affected. "Never even considered it."

Except every other day and twice a day on PMS week.

"Those memories kept me warm on many a lonely night." He looked me up and down leaving a trail of heat. And all that burgeoning heat pissed me off. How dare he once-over me? And how dare he use my memories for his sick pleasure? My memories. My sick pleasure. Fucking confusion.

I sighed. Enough was enough. "What do you want, Finn?"

He shook his head and chuckled. "I don't even know how to say this."

Oh, dear God. "Just say it."

My voice cracking in the middle absolutely did *not* mean I was hoping he'd ask to fuck his way down memory lane.

He smiled and reached out as if he planned to touch me. I moved back. "Always so tough."

Yeah. That was right. I was too tough to be hung up on

a guy who waited just long enough for the going to get tough before he got the hell out of Glouster.

"I'm busy, Finn." I swept my arm toward the mountain of Christmas decorations I'd liberated from their attic exile. The city had already sent me a letter for breeching my agreement with them. And now it was either hang the lights by Christmas Eve or pay the $1,000 fine to make up for the tax break I got when I refinanced.

"Right." Now he wouldn't look at me and my stomach churned. I'd seen this whole routine before, and it hadn't ended well for me. His Adam's apple bobbed once then again. "I'm engaged."

Oh shit.

"That's great." I lied and hid behind a fuck-you smile as my body clenched in anger, maybe even regret. It was also stupid of me to continue standing there staring at my love-life past when I had Christmas future to hate. I opened a box and stared at the little houses inside that belonged to the perfect Christmas town. Oh, yeah. This box could wait until last.

"Lis."

His voice, or more the softness of it, cut me. Deep. That had to be where the tears came from.

"What?" I couldn't think of anything else to say.

"There's more."

Well, of course, there was more. Why wouldn't there be? Otherwise, he could've handled this news with an invitation, or an announcement sent through the US Postal Service. "Okay."

One-word answers in a squeaky tone were about all I could manage.

"Our divorce is…apparently, we're still married. After I signed them and sent them back, did you file the papers?"

My mouth dropped open. He was accusing me? Making this my fault? "Of course, I filed the papers."

The ones he'd *mailed* back to me. I'd opened them and a bottle of tequila at the same time, but I clearly remembered waking up early, rolling out of bed, throwing up…everything else was a blur but I would've never hung onto them considering how badly I wanted him to know I wanted to be free of him. I had to have filed them. And no way in hell did I burn those papers in the fireplace. That part had been a dream. A weird little drunken dream.

Oh shit.

"So, we're still married?"

He ran his hands through his hair.

"I'm supposed to get married on Christmas Eve." But if I had to give my opinion under oath in a court, I would have had to say he didn't look so happy or excited about it. "I'm supposed to be spending Christmas in Hawaii. With my wife."

"Awesome. I just got a new swimsuit, it was on clearance online…" And my laughter might have been inappropriate considering this was probably, I was willing to admit to about ninety-four percent certain, my fault.

"Oh relax. You can still marry her. It just won't be official yet." He shot me a glare, and I rolled my eyes in response. "Don't worry. Your little St. Nick is still gonna get his jolly in Paradise. We just have to go to the courthouse tomorrow. We'll talk to the judge and I'll explain. They're very sympathetic around here to stupid mistakes. Remember?"

Okay. That part was just nasty. "We'll get divorced in time for your wedding. Don't worry."

"It's going to be that easy, huh?" He cocked one eyebrow over the eyes I'd never gotten over and I could've swooned.

But didn't. "It was that easy to get married, right?"

One Decade Ago

MOST DAYS I felt lucky that I answered the ad Sofia Marks hung in the student union for a roommate. Today was not one of those days. She was on her kick again. The Felicity had no life kick. No friends besides her kick. No fun little one-night stands with fraternity boys kick.

I couldn't argue because I didn't drink or smoke, and I was always home on school nights tucked into bed at a very respectable 11:30. And as chancellor of Glouster University, my dad couldn't have been prouder, but Sofia made fun of these attributes like they were afflictions. And today I was with her. Today, I wanted the college experience. I wanted to act out. Sow a wild oat, for once in my life.

Sofia Marks was a vlog goddess with hundreds of thousands of followers who stuck around to find out her opinions and to see what pranks and stunts she might pull at any given time. She didn't follow a schedule, didn't have a category of topics she followed, and didn't have any sort of filter as far as what opinions she expressed. But people loved her. Funny. Pretty. Intelligent. All the best adjectives fit her. Plus, she was blonde, built like a stripper, and had no lack of nightlife or party life or life in general. Our friendship and the fact we'd become so close defied all logic.

"I'm just saying," and she'd been saying it for the last hour and a half, "that you spend so much time studying and trying to please your daddy that you have missed out on one of the great college experiences. It's our senior year, Felicity, live a little, for once."

I hardly thought of hooking up with a frat boy as one of the great college experiences, but what did I know? And today, she was preaching to the very bored, very enthusiastic choir. "All right, then. Let's do this."

"Ah, grasshopper. Nothing is as simple as I make it seem." She'd already dressed me in jeans tight enough the world could see…my thoughts, and a shirt short enough my sheer lace bra threatened to play peek-a-boo if I so much as lifted my arm to my shoulder, and boots with a heel that could be used as a lethal weapon.

"We need to finesse this situation." She held her phone out in front of her as if she was selfie-ing. "And today's Kiss cam feature is my beautiful, and oh-so-charming best friend."

She angled the phone toward me. "World, this is Felicity. Felicity, say hi to the world."

I waved. "Hello, world."

My enthusiasm, however, hit the skids and began to fade as it misted into a fine vapor. But I pasted on my best smile and crinkled my fingers at her camera like I was all in. Because if I didn't, we'd end up reshooting this scene a couple hundred times until I cooperated. Until the butterflies in my belly turned to rabid bats and I passed out from the stress of this whole thing. How she got me to agree to this, I would never know.

"And the unsuspecting subject of today's segment is...," She let the camera pan the area then turned to me and smiled. "Oh, girl. Are you ever in luck today?"

She pinched the screen to zoom in on her target. "A genius with a jockstrap. That's right, ladies and gentlemen. Today's subject is the much sought-after Finn Makenzie. Tall, handsome, born to delight the ladies with his adorable smile, his uber-sexy charm, and his super big..."

The pause was intentional and suggestive. She certainly knew how to lead her audience on. "...brain."

She smiled that come-hither smile, and I knew the masses hithered.

"Ordinarily, I would have my bestie making the day of a Dungeons and Dragons half-vampire, but this is a woman who has denied herself the joys of college, the frat parties, the frat *guys*." She winked big and exaggerated.

"She's missed all the fun that can be found on a university campus. And since this is her last year at the illustrious school that can't be named thanks to the fuddy-duddy board of chancellors here at one of Maine's," extra emphasis there, "most prestigious universities we're going to fix that."

Over the last few months, the university demanded she stop giving out her location because once or twice, she might have earned herself a stalker that showed up on campus. Turned out, internet fame was dangerous.

But so was walking up to a stranger and kissing him without warning or a word of approval before the unrequested and possibly unwanted with potential for rejection lip-smacking. Still, that was the plan for this afternoon.

And had the kissee to my kisser been anonymous, my stomach wouldn't have had a thousand or so of the previously mentioned butterflies working together to beat their way to escape. And my head wouldn't have been swimming with just the idea of walking across the lawn to be close enough to see him.

Finn sat about 20 yards away, on the rim of the fountain, sun shining on his golden hair making it look almost blonde with his eyes hidden behind a pair of aviator sunglasses. Oblivious. Reading. His focus on anything but me and Sofia.

She gave me a shove in the back, and I stumbled then turned to her. Oh yeah. She got the whole thing on camera. So, my only option for redemption was to hold my head high, march up to him, and lay a kiss on him that made his world spin while I remained obviously unaffected and stone-faced. "Here I go."

I didn't stutter step or trip. I didn't fall into his lap. I didn't do any more to embarrass myself than to stop in front of him and wait.

The deal was, I couldn't speak. Had to just go in for the kiss and hope he wasn't the kind of guy who swung first and asked questions later. Also had to hope there wasn't some crazy girlfriend, Sofia would know if he had one, I hoped, waiting to stomp me a new ass crack.

As soon as I tugged him to his feet, I realized my mistake. I'd underestimated how his height coupled with my short stature would affect my ability to make this happen. I should have just leaned in and planted the kiss. Damn. Now it was going to look wonky on film. I would look like a novice. Like I'd never been kissed. Desperate. Needy. Inexperienced.

I had to save this moment. Had to make it look like I had some kind of clue. I channeled Sofia. She always knew exactly what to do. She would slide her palm up his chest to tangle in his hair. Then she'd nudge him down, close her eyes, and press her lips against his.

At least, that was what I did. And holy, holy, holy shit. His lips were soft as they caressed mine and his arms strong when he wrapped them around me and nestled my body as close to his as I could get without actually being inside his clothes with him. And this kiss lasted…forever and not nearly long enough. He used his tongue to trace the seam of my lips and whether I intended it or not, and I would take that information to my grave, my mouth opened, and his tongue slid against mine.

My knees went weak and warmth curled through me from my belly outward to my fingertips and my toes and the ends of my hair. There wasn't a single part of me that didn't want to rub against him while I purred like a satisfied kitten.

Nothing in my life had ever felt better. Nothing. Not a single thing. In my life. Ever. Probably never would.

He pulled back. "If that's what being your study buddy is like, I'm going to need a copy of your class schedule so I can sign up for all your classes."

I smiled. Still, by kiss cam rule, which incidentally I found appalling, not allowed to speak. Instead, I turned and walked away. Tripped three steps out. Landed on my chest, my chin, and my hands while my legs did some crazy scorpion thing and ended up with my feet somehow smacking the back of my head. I knew because the video of that fall was my first foray into internet fame when it went viral. Although it wouldn't be my last.

3

Finn

y choice for accommodations came down to a bed and breakfast that doubled as a dairy farm and smelled like it, or a chain motel outside of town. Neither place cared that I was a doctor, or that my future wife was a talk-show host. There was no impressing anybody, these days, it seemed.

I pondered the choices presented to me, but really, all I could think about was how close to nonexistent the sliver of hope was that I could get back together with the woman that was still my wife. That weighed on my mind heavily.

My dilemma became even more bleak when I learned an awful truth. Neither of my choices for accommodation had…accommodation available.

The Santa Claus convention for the greater east coast was in town, with only a few days left until Christmas Eve, and the manager at the chain motel didn't want to kick a

Santa from his room. She might end up on the naughty list. She actually said that to me as I stared at her bleakly.

I drove to my final option, one that hadn't changed a bit in the decade I'd been gone. Well, it changed a little. The same sofa sat in front of flat screens the size of the walls they hung on and the same tables held a new tower of beer cans since ours was demolished right around the time everything else fell down around us. The place still smelled like stale booze, smoke, and sweat socks, though.

No way could I stay there. I walked out and drove to a bar. There wouldn't be anyone there I knew, and that suited me fine.

I didn't want to admit how seeing Felicity again affected me. Seeing her made my guts twist and my heart ache. So much time had passed and, eventually, I'd learned how not to think of her. How to shield myself when some woman I passed on the street wore Felicity's perfume or had hair with the same sun-streaked color or had big blue eyes.

Today, she undid all of it. Well, actually, I did since I couldn't blame her for all the reactions that went through me when I saw her again. I could try to drink them away though, which is exactly what I did. With a guy who'd lost his job.

"Fired after 27 years." He shook his head and stared down into his whiskey. "At Christmas."

"Hard time to be unemployed." I could be sympathetic.

"And in town for Christmas with the wife's family and her perfect sister, Cheryl." He nodded and downed his drink then motioned for another. "And her perfect husband, Chip or Skip or Joe." He glanced at me. "Tell you the truth, she goes through 'em like my wife goes through purses." His laugh, a loud guffaw of noise, tumbled through the emptiness of the bar. "You got a wife, kid?"

Well…

"Yeah." That was the truth. I definitely had a wife. A beautiful, smart, funny, sexy wife. "I do have a wife."

"You ever have to tell her you got canned five days before Christmas because you took a trip with her, one she demanded you take, by the way, when you didn't have the time off to take?" In the bad situation game, he won. But it wasn't going to stop me from crying into my beer later. In the car. Where I'd be sleeping.

"Can't say that I have." But if he wanted to play the who had it worse game, I wanted my turn. "But, have you ever been…"

I laid out the whole situation.

By the time I finished, he had wide eyes, an open mouth, and a new drink for each of us. I took a long sip, okay, a big drink, while he continued to stare at me.

"Okay." He nodded once. "Okay. Here's what you do."

His eyes flicked closed then opened and closed and opened again a couple more times as if he needed to blink to work out his words before he spoke again. "You march over there, don't drive. Cops here are dicks about DUI. You march over to your house, you have just as much right to that house as her, so that has to mean something."

He picked up momentum with each word. And I didn't bother to tell him she would kill me for staking any claim on that house. "Anyway, you march over there. You walk in like you own the place and you demand to sleep in the bed with your wife."

When I opened my mouth to object because it didn't take a genius to know how that would go with Felicity, he held up his hand. "She's the one who didn't sign the papers or file, or whatever it was that happened. You did your part."

Maybe it was because I was drunk that I agreed, or maybe because he was absolutely, one hundred percent, without a doubt right, I had signed and sent the papers back to her. It was on her if we were still married. And maybe it wasn't subconscious. Maybe it was…her missing *all this*. And by *all this* I meant me. "That's right. I did my part."

"Of course, it could be clerical." He shrugged one shoulder and finished the drink in front of him.

Aghast, I stared at him, mouth open, brow crinkled. "No. No."

And though all my head shaking wasn't good for my equilibrium, I continued. "No. No. Not clerkical."

Okay, clerkical wasn't a word, but I couldn't get the right one out. "This is Flisty wanting me back."

Something changed in my new buddy, and his eyes narrowed. I stumbled back a step and stared at my new BFF with confusion.

Now he was all devil's advocate, and I was in danger of getting my ass kicked in a bar fight I was about six seconds from starting?

"Then why'd it take you ten years to find out? If she wanted you and that's why, how come she didn't call you?"

"What?" Didn't matter. I was back, and she was my wife and by heck, that's how we were meant to be. I knew it since I first held her and kissed her and…

One Decade Ago

SHE HAD fire dancing in her eyes. And I could feel the heat from her anger. We were halfway between the diner and her house, and it didn't take an expert in all things Felicity, which I'd become over the last three weeks, to know something was wrong. More than once during dinner, she'd taken my hand and laid it on her leg, her bare leg thanks to the shortest skirt I'd ever seen her wear. She sat closer. Rubbed her breasts against my arm, six times, as we walked from the movie to the restaurant then four more times in the last three blocks. She'd even worn heels, mile-high heels that made her legs look even longer. Legs I pictured more than once wrapped around my waist. Legs I wanted to kiss from ankle to thigh.

I stopped walking a second after I realized she'd let go of my arm and was standing a few feet back. I turned to face her. "What's wrong?"

"I don't know, Finn. You tell me." She stared up at me, a glare on her face, as she planted her arms on her hips. "You're the *easiest* guy on campus, everybody says so, until I want to get laid. Then all of a sudden, you're practically a monk."

What? "What the hell are you talking about?"

Because if she was saying she wanted to have sex, then I

was down for that, I was totally down for that. I could be naked in less than three seconds if she was so inclined, public street or not.

"I'm talking about the clothes and these fucking shoes." She reached down and flipped open the buckle on the sexiest shoe I'd ever seen then stepped out. She repeated the process with the twin sexy shoe and then picked them up by the strap and shook them at me. "These are the most painful shoes in the world, but I wore them because Sofia said no guy can resist fuck-me shoes."

She huffed out an angry breath. "But obviously, she never met Finn-sex-with-everyone-but-Felicity-Makenzie."

"Felicity…" I wanted to tell her how wrong she was. How I'd been taking matters into my own hands before *and* after every single one of our dates because I'd never wanted anyone more than I wanted her.

"Am I not pretty enough? Or slutty enough? Or what?" And I almost died when her eyes filled with tears and her voice wavered on her next words. "Oh, forget it."

As she turned to storm away, I slipped my fingers through hers and tugged her back. "Hey."

She sniffed and looked down at her shoes in her free hand.

"Hey." I curled my finger under her chin and nudged until she lifted her eyes to meet mine. "You are…"

Who was I kidding? I didn't have the right words. I wasn't poetic or romantic. Most of my deepest thoughts came immediately after the organ directly below my belt blasted off from its happy place.

I kissed her instead. Slow and deep. So sensual it wasn't going to be long until we were ass high in my deepest thoughts. Her hands tangled in my hair and held me as if there was a chance in hell I'd try to pull away.

Her lips were like silk, and her soft whimper when I deepened the kiss urged me on. Made me want more and I already wanted so much.

What I didn't want to do was push and make her do something because she thought I wanted it. But I also didn't have the kind of willpower to stop kissing her. To plan something special for us. Instead, I pulled her toward the frat house and Keaton's car.

Taking her back to the frat house wasn't an option since it was a Friday night and there would be a party raging. Her place was out, since her dad was the school's chancellor, and I needed my scholarship. And no way could I manage to show her how I felt about her in the backseat of a Mustang. But along with his fancy car, Keaton also had an extremely fancy boat, a party boat. It was the *ultimate* party boat, with a fully stocked fridge, a big screen TV, and mirrors on the bedroom ceiling. And since I was on the injured list and not required to travel with the team, all of whom were in Oregon tonight for tomorrow's game, it would be empty.

She didn't ask me where I was taking her, or who the car belonged to. She just climbed into the car and held my hand as I drove. No nerves. Which was okay because I had enough for both of us. I had a huge case of the insecurities, of the *please, don't let me blow this* kind. And yeah, I knew there was a joke in there. One too crass to make about a girl like Felicity. Probably about any girl, but definitely about the one smiling at me as I led her down the dock to the boat before I helped her aboard.

She didn't wait for me but walked to the far end of the deck, where we partied when we took the boat out. Where the canvas chairs were lined along the side. Where I'd spent many a summer "fishing trip" getting lucky without a fishing pole in sight.

As she leaned over the rail, I walked behind her and waited. I had a hand on the rail on each side of her and it would've been so easy to slide closer, rub against her, but I held back. This night had to be perfect.

She pulled my arms around her so that my hands rested on her stomach, and then she breathed in deep and blew it out slow. "This is so pretty."

"You're so pretty." And I was so lame, but it was the first thing I'd thought, and it was true. When she turned to face me with a look on her face, *that* look, being lame didn't matter so much.

She slid her hands up my chest and rested them on my shoulders where her thumbs could stroke my throat, then she lifted on her tip toes and pressed a line of kisses along my jaw as I wrapped my arms around her waist and tugged, so our bodies lined up, chest to chest, belly to belly and hip to hip. And my body buzzed everywhere we touched.

"Show me the rest?"

Anything she wanted. Anytime. Anyplace. Somehow, I'd managed to fall for her. That made everything else so simple and so complicated. But for tonight...

We walked into the kitchen and bar area.

"Galley." I pointed to the seating across from the bar. "More party area."

I pointed to the steps on the right that curved around to the bedroom under this room. "That's how you get to the guest room. Bunk beds."

I had no idea about boat terminology. "And this way…" I pointed to the other set of steps. "Goes to the master bedroom."

I looked at the refrigerator. "Thirsty?"

When she shook her head no, my mouth simply refused to comply and let my body take the lead. It wanted to go straight to the bedroom, so I hauled back on the reins my body wanted to run away with. Take it slow, I reminded myself and ran through a menu of food. "Hungry? There's sandwich stuff, and meat I could throw on the grill."

What?

She smiled. Crooked her finger. Looked up at me from under her lashes with her chin tilted down. "Come here."

And now I didn't care if we had an entire team from Top Chef and all the fancy dishes they made sitting in the kitchen behind me. I didn't have enough blood left in my brain to care about more than the woman standing right in front of me, inviting me to take her to bed. She didn't speak, didn't do more than smile and lead me down the steps and through the hallway to the bedroom.

I followed her. I couldn't imagine doing anything else.

She slid the door open and walked inside. "Holy shit."

Oh yeah. I'd had the same reaction the first time I saw it too. The bed on its pedestal, three steps above the floor.

The soft lighting. The windows that looked out at the ocean. The deep blue satin sheets and silver comforter that rustled when she sat on the bed. The water lapping against the side of the boat and the soft hum of the fan that forced air through the vents were the only sounds other than her soft breathing and the pounding of my heart in my ears.

"Music?" I motioned to the sound system on the wall, and she nodded. Chances were one of the presets would be some kind of sexy jazz that could play in the background, but I couldn't find it. I found rap with a heavy bass line, then some country. I groaned when the next station was a rock station with screaming guitars and anthem beats. She pulled out her phone, swiped a couple of screens then set it on the table. With the softest, sexiest smile any human being could ever produce, she stood and took the remote control to set beside her phone. Then she pulled me close again.

"I want you, Finn. I've been thinking about it and dreaming about it," she shoved my shirt up and over my head then tossed it behind her. "I even named my vibrator after you, so I'd be calling out your name."

She flicked the button at my waistband open while I closed my eyes and enjoyed the brush of her hands against my skin coupled with the vision of her alone in her room, a room I'd never seen but imagined now, on her bed, pleasuring herself while she called out for me. "You still with me, Finn?"

I opened my eyes and smiled down at her. With her? "Oh yeah. Right here."

I lifted the hem of her shirt, slid my hands along her

ribs as I inched it over her skin, and sucked in a hard breath when I realized there was no bra and my palm brushed along the side of her breast. Oh fuck. I'd never been so turned on, so into a moment, so ready to…

And then she was bare, her hands shoving my pants away, and I couldn't move. I couldn't stop looking at her. I couldn't stop wanting her. She was beautiful. Perfect. So… everything. And I wanted her. Wanted her enough to kick my jeans away and lift her so that our bare skin touched from shoulder to waist and thigh to thigh. When she wrapped her legs around my waist, ground her pussy against my dick as that tiny little skirt slipped up to her waist and I found out she wasn't wearing panties either, I was gone.

Tonight, nothing mattered in the world but Felicity. And for as long as I lived, I would hope tonight never ended.

4

Felicity

"That's dope!" Sofia, who'd started all this with her kiss cam ten years ago, pulled her bottom lip between her teeth while she still managed to sneer, and shook her hands at me.

"No." I shook my head at her latest attempt in the campaign to find herself and her "catchphrase." But I was patient because that was what friends did. "Could you please pick this afternoon's personality? I need your help."

I hadn't started to panic yet, but the heart flutters, the trembling hands, and the churning in my stomach said I was either headed for a panic attack or something that would require wet wipes and antacids. Hence the emergency call to my best and only friend.

She flopped into the chair beside my sofa and kicked her "kicks" onto my coffee table as she adjusted two-grand in fake jewelry. "I'm not climbing on a roof and helping you hang Christmas lights. You're the one who couldn't bear to move off Main Street in case you know who came back. You deal with the city managers and their ridiculous fines."

"I don't need your help hanging Christmas lights." I had far more pressing issues than my agreement with the city. "I need you to help me figure out why I'm freaking out over you know who."

And in case she wasn't sure who we were talking about, I whispered, "Finn."

Sofia had known both of us since before we became an "us", she just knew me better. "He came here today."

"You know who showed up here?" Her perfectly sculpted, and I do mean sculpted, eyebrow arched in shock.

I nodded and she sat up, braced her feet onto the floor, and dropped her mouth open. Now I had her attention. "Oh shit."

She nodded twice.

"Okay. All right." More nodding. "Is this a pizza and ice cream situation or should we go straight for the vodka cranberry to deal with the ex-husband situation?"

My skin went hot. Not just hot. Blazing. An inferno of white heat rolling from my forehead to my toes and back again. Maybe it was the memory of the eleven glorious and seventy-percent naked days I'd spent as his wife. Not glorious or naked enough to keep him, but...whether it was that or my inexplicable and equally flaming embarrassment, I could've fried eggs on my skin and served them up with a side of toast and bacon. But I glanced at her.

Almost too embarrassed to look at her. I'd fucked up on a grand scale. I had to correct her and didn't want to. But I did it. "Current husband."

She cocked an eyebrow. "Oh, shit. Houston, we have a tequila situation."

She went to the kitchen like a woman on a mission and came back with the emergency bottle of Cuervo I kept, usually for *her* emergencies. She poured me a shot, gestured for me to drink, waited quietly while I did, then sat back again. "Go."

I shook my head as a picture of Finn, with the beautiful face, the eyes, the body, popped into my head. Why couldn't I just hate him like a real ex-wife? He left me, broke my heart, and yet the lust was real. "He looks good."

She nodded, blonde ponytail bobbing.

"Of course, he does." She took another drink. "Go on."

"And he smells good." Like citrus with hints of cinnamon and mint.

"You sniffed him? Oh, Fliss." She sighed disappointed, and I widened my eyes, unused to being the unhinged one in our relationship.

"No. He hugged me." With those gloriously strong arms at my waist, his broad chest under my cheek, he achieved hug perfection. At which time there might have been some sniffing.

"He hugged you?" She looked me up and down from my red bandana, dusty overalls, and worn sneakers. Okay. I needed a shower, but I wasn't near to scaring small children yet.

"Yeah." I wanted to savor the thought, but she jerked her body forward and stared at me with wide eyes.

"And you didn't immediately drag him into the bed and wash away that wicked dry spell you've been having? Maybe rekindle all those loving feelings?" She refilled my glass.

"No." We toasted, drank, refilled, and repeated. I had a lot more news to go.

"Good. Good." She nodded her approval. "Waiting until he left to pleasure yourself was a much better way to go. No emotional attachment."

And the approval turned to disappointment.

But I'd waited until he left then called her. There'd been no pleasure. Not then. Not now. "Sofia, no."

"You did it while he was here?" She took a swig straight from the bottle. "Bold."

She swiped the back of her hand over her mouth. "But I get it."

Seriously, I needed counsel. Advice. Her special brand of man-wisdom. But in her defense, I hadn't managed to tell her the part about him being engaged. Probably info she needed before we figured out what to do. In my defense, I didn't think she would have been drinking on a night when she didn't have a date. Although, in hindsight, I probably should've asked how much she'd had before I sent up the SOS flare, then commenced to Cuervo-ing my afternoon away.

"I don't even know why we're friends." I snatched the bottle and took a giant gulp.

"I know. I totally would've slept with him first then

freaked out later." She shook off whatever thought was going through her head, probably a Finn fantasy I should've hated her for. "Okay. So, here's what we know. He looks good."

I nodded and she tapped her finger against her chin. "And he smells good."

Another nod.

"And you didn't have sex with him?" She asked it quickly, as if to make sure I wasn't fibbing.

"No." I crossed my arms over my chest, bottle pressed into my ribs. I didn't want to share my Cuervo anymore.

She took the bottle back, and I waited until she pressed it to her lips. Because news like mine was best digested along with a big glug of alcohol. "And it's my fault we're still married. I think I burned the divorce papers instead of filing them."

She took the bottle, drank then passed it back to me. "Shut up."

"And he's engaged to someone else."

"Oh fuck." She took another drink, hugged the bottle to her chest, looking more needy than I felt. And that said something since I was about six seconds from rolling into a ball and whimpering until I lost consciousness from either hyperventilation or drunkenness. "Did you burn them on purpose?"

"What?" Of course, I did. But I wasn't to the point I could admit it to either of us.

"You were pretty...crazy when you got them in the mail." She took a swig and hugged the bottle. "I mean, no one would've blamed you. Hell, no one would now, either."

She shrugged one shoulder and twisted her lips to one side. "Except maybe Finn. And his fiancée."

Fiancée? Whoever she was…I hated her.

We passed the bottle back and forth a couple times, but instead of numbing me to the flares of attraction to Finn that I couldn't escape because my mind had too vivid memories of him in various…positions in my house, the tequila made my lust shine brighter and bigger.

"So, he looked good, huh?"

"Oh yeah." I picked up my phone, inspired. "I should call him, right?"

Because…tequila.

I poised my finger, let it hover over the keypad to dial random numbers since I didn't have his. Thankfully, she snatched it away, but drunk me had a plan. "I'll just send him a telepathic message."

Which wouldn't have worked had I not pointed my index finger at the center of my forehead while I closed my eyes and stood on one foot. As soon as the message left my mind on its cosmic journey to his, I giggled as I yanked the door open, not because anyone knocked or rang the bell, but because I was drunk and telepathic.

I turned to look out the door and my eyes went wide. "Holy shit. I'm telepathic."

Finn stood on the porch in the same outfit as this afternoon, the same smile I'd fallen in love with all those years ago.

"I didn't think the hotel would be booked, so I didn't make a reservation." He frowned. "Turns out, bad plan."

Sofia leaned over my shoulder for her first look at him in ten years. "Holy shit. You are so psychic."

She stage whispered, "And you're right. He's still hot."

I turned with every intention to shoot her a supersonic death glare, but I ended up nodding. "I know, right?"

But I had Finn standing on my front porch, technically *our* front porch since we were still married, and I'd fully supported the community property part of our marriage once upon a time. "Hang on. I should figure out what's going on here."

I turned back to Finn, once again struck by how attractive he was. "Wow. Just…wow."

He leaned in and sniffed, and I covered my mouth with my hand. "Have you been drinking, Lis?"

To lie or not to lie. I couldn't anyway, because hearing the way he said my name, or the half of it he'd always used, sent a shiver over my skin. "Don't judge. I'm having a really weird day."

He chuckled, and I swayed toward him because the sound was better than anything I'd heard except Finn saying my name. Of all the things I'd forgotten, how had Finn Makenzie's laugh made the list? Deep. Resonant. Memorable in ways most other sounds were not.

"Me, too." He nodded toward his duffle bag. "The, um, east coast Santa convention is in town, and they're taking up all the rooms at the hotel. I don't have anywhere to stay."

How was I supposed to know what he meant when he let his tongue slide over his lower lip and his head tilt. All I could see were visions of Finn coming in for a kiss that led to a touch that led to all the human contact, male human, things I'd been missing.

"And you want to stay here?" *Yes, please!*

Sofia leaned over my shoulder and gave me a hard shake as she, again, stage whispered, "Bad idea. Horrible. Run to the closet and hide. I'll handle this."

She jerked my shoulder and moved to stand in front of me. But, tonight, I didn't need protection. I needed…Finn.

And if I hadn't enjoyed being so near Finn, smelling his cologne, seeing his eyes, I wouldn't have jockeyed for position and we wouldn't have ended up falling out the door onto Finn's luggage while I screamed at her.

"Get out of my way!"

She yelled, "I'm not letting you have sex with him!"

I rolled over to hold her down when two arms slid around my waist and lifted me off my best friend so I bicycle-kicked through the air. Then as Sofia stood, I slowed down, exaggerating every motion until we both laughed. And he set me on my feet.

Sofia narrowed her eyes and balled her fists. If not for the tequila, I would've moved to protect him. Also, if not for the tequila, she would have aimed better, and I wouldn't have been unprepared and her punch wouldn't have landed in my face, my left eye specifically.

I went down hard, skinned my knee, and probably broke a rib when she landed on top of me. Again. "Oh God, Lissy. I'm so sorry. I meant to hit the jackass."

She pushed off me and sat back on her heels. "You know, the slimeball jackass who just waltzed back in here on a cloud of Old Spice or some shit, looking all fresh and tight, making you want to play the slap and tickle game."

Even drunk, I knew this was bad. "Sofia. Stop. Do they even make Old Spice anymore?"

I looked at Finn who shrugged. And even though she was talking smack about him, he smiled like he understood. Or maybe I imagined it because I'd spent so many long nights fantasizing about and remembering that smile. "He smells like spice and citrus. And sex. He smells like I want to have sex."

That didn't come out right. Didn't come out entirely wrong either. And he smiled again or maybe still, so a little humiliation was worth it.

"Stop picturing him naked." Oh, she knew me so well, and real-life Finn looked just as damned good as imaginary Finn, and imaginary Finn had been the kick starter to many a sweaty midsummer night alone with my vibrator.

Sofia stood and wiped herself off as if I hadn't broken her fall and kept her from getting so much as a speck of dust on her outfit. "Jerk face, here, should know what he does to you. How you haven't had a real relationship in ten years because you can't get over him. And how unfair it is that you haven't had an orgasm that wasn't self-induced since college."

"Oh shit." My mouth dropped open. Tequila made Sofia's secret vault spring open. I needed damage control, to save face. To not want him to take responsibility to rectify that last one. I looked at him. "Um, flergh."

He chewed his lower lip, probably to hide a smile, but I was too drunk to know the difference.

"Can't just make up words, Lis." He glanced at Sofia then at me. "Don't worry. You aren't going to remember this tomorrow."

And that would've been consolation enough…"But you will."

He grinned and helped me up then kept hold of my hand, brought it to his lips, and pressed a kiss against my knuckles as he looked up at me from under his lashes. "Oh yeah."

Because I couldn't stand there staring at my engaged husband and maintain any sort of self-respect, I turned to Sofia. "I'm going to get started on the forgetting." I kissed her cheek. "Don't drive home. Stay or Uber."

I had things to forget. So, so many things.

One Decade Ago

THERE WAS no graceful way to get out of there. Not that I hadn't done a walk of shame before, but I was on a boat, a yacht, with Finn Makenzie, who knew his way around not only my body but a boat kitchen.

He set a plate in front of me where I sat at a counter that doubled as a table. "It's not much."

It was an omelet with vegetables and cheese and goodness served to me by a bare-chested guy, bare-chested because I was wearing his shirt. And it was perfect. The omelet, the boat, the sun rising over the ocean, Finn Makenzie's unbuttoned jeans. Everything was perfect.

And to be honest, I didn't care about the omelet. Or the

boat. Or the sun. I only cared about Finn. I wanted to know everything. All the little details that made him who he was…which just so happened to be more perfect than any guy I'd ever met.

"When's your birthday?"

He squinted, then cocked his head and smiled. "January." After a second, he added, "10th. When's yours?"

"October 29th." I shrugged. "I always had Halloween birthday parties. One year I went as a woodchuck, but everyone thought I was a groundhog, and every day until Christmas someone managed to find a way to ask me if I saw my own shadow." Stop it with the too much information.

He chuckled. "That's cute."

And that was all he said. Didn't elaborate with a cute little anecdote of his own. What he did was better. He took my fork, used the side to slice off a piece of the omelet then fed it to me. And as divine as it was, literally melt in my mouth goodness, it only took a second to realize that I wanted more than the religious experience of kissing him, sex with him, and now being fed by him provided.

"What was your favorite Halloween costume?" I was at my flirty best. Chest puffed out onto the counter. Eyelashes freshly mascara-ed and batting at optimal speed for attractive. Tongue swiping along lower lip with flawless precision.

And he turned away. Back to the stove, then to the sink with the skillet in hand. "I didn't really…Halloween wasn't my thing."

Oh. And someone who hadn't spent the last few weeks

memorizing every expression, etching into my brain what each tone of voice meant wouldn't have known I upset him. But I wasn't just anyone. I'd sponged up all the things about him he probably didn't realize then all the things he probably did.

"Finn?"

"I didn't spend a lot of time in one place." He turned to look at me, but leaned back against the counter, letting it stand between us as the physical manifestation of the mental wall I wanted to bust down. But I didn't know what question to ask or if I should say anything. I stared instead. Creepy stared. Because no matter what I told myself, I knew I should say something. Something profound that let him know I was here, not judging, not pitying, just here. For him. But I managed zero words.

"My parents died when I was seven and I got bounced around from family member to family member. Wasn't much time for Halloween costumes." He didn't look at me, he looked at the floor, and my heart melted for him as my throat tried to choke me to death.

Not quite a woodchuck story, but so much more than I expected. This was deep and meaningful. This was…real. Not that I'd made up the woodchuck story but this one had a depth mine didn't. I stood and walked around the counter to hug him. "We'll make up for it."

He wrapped his arms around me and laid his cheek on top of my head as I listened to the steady beat of his heart.

"Every day from now on." And I meant it. Because somewhere along the line I fell for Finn Makenzie. "I see a whole mess of matching costumes in your future, mister."

"I love you, Felicity." He tilted my head up and looked deep into my eyes. And I'd read enough romance novels and seen plenty enough rom-coms to know there were only three words I could say back and the three-second rule wasn't just for dropped food. It applied here, too.

"I love you, too." And if I sounded breathless and needy and desperate, it was because I wanted to make sure he knew I was for real. I didn't add *so much* because his mouth brushed against mine and there wasn't room for words.

This time when he carried me to the bedroom, when he moved onto the bed beside me, when he kissed me, I knew in my soul that Finn Makenzie was the man I wanted for the rest of my life.

5

Finn

In the last ten years, it had never occurred to me that I would ever wake up in this house again. Smelling her perfume on the borrowed pillow or seeing her shoes neatly lined beside the door. Hearing her voice, faded and in the distance, cursing.

I sat up on the blue denim sofa that could've used some serious breaking in. I held my breath and listened.

"Son of a bitch!" Sounded like she was outside, yet… above me?

In short, on the roof. I pulled on my jeans and a t-shirt then a jacket not nearly heavy enough for the wind blowing in off the ocean. When I opened the back door and saw the ladder lying on the ground across the yard and resting on the short fence, my heart attempted a speedy escape through my throat, and I risked a glance up to where a string of lights dangled over the gutter.

"Lis?" The only sound in the backyard was the wind. But I'd already heard her, knew she was up there. Or I would've been more freaked at the evidence around me. I moved the ladder back in place and climbed. She straddled the peak of the roof, holding a ball of tangled lights in front of her. "What are you doing?"

She motioned to the lights and shrugged.

"I tried wrinkling my nose and wishing, but it didn't work." She wrinkled her nose and moved it around, then frowned. "Might've even made the knot bigger."

I nodded as if finding Felicity on the roof, probably hungover and sporting a black eye that looked painful, was completely normal. Expected even. "You could hire someone."

She threw her head back and laughed, although I suspected it was more from hysteria, maybe hypothermia, since she'd only worn a hoodie, jeans, a scarf, and a pair of bright orange work gloves to climb up there. "No need. Can't you see I have this all under control?"

And as if to emphasize the opposite of her point, when she waved her hand, she let go of the ball of lights and it rolled down the rooftop to somersault over the edge and thunk onto the lawn. She sighed. "Well, that's unfortunate."

"And the ladder?" Same old me. I wanted her to need me. Or to at least say she needed me.

"Wind." When I tilted my head, she rolled her eyes. "Fine. I accidentally kicked it when I stepped around it."

She clucked her tongue against her teeth and waved a hand again. "Oh, please. There are hours of daylight left. It wasn't time to panic yet. Besides, Mrs. Ellerby will be out walking Pookie around lunchtime. She'd call the fire department for me if I asked."

She pulled her phone out of her hoodie pocket, then watched as it flipped out of her hands and slid down the roof to land beside the ball of lights on the ground.

"Or I could have called 911." She stared down at her phone. "By standing on the roof and yelling *911! 911!*"

I grinned because we both knew she would've ended up calling me. And I was glad for it even though I assumed it was the reason she frowned.

"What are you doing up here, Finn?" She sighed, her head cocked to the right.

"The house, the lights…not your problem. So… shouldn't you be downstairs all snuggled in bed?" Her face went red, could've been the cold, or not. "On the couch?"

A picture of Beth and her ridiculous middle-of-the-night text message filtered through my mind.

Sorry. Didn't mean to interrupt your happy time on Nerds Getting Nasty, but you've been there since yesterday and I haven't gotten a divorce update yet. So…?

"We need to, um, get to the courthouse." And now I felt like jumping off the roof.

"Right." She straightened, but the hand fluttering that signaled her nerves started. "Of course."

She threw her leg over to the backside of the roof and stood to walk down the pitch like she was an old pro.

And maybe because I didn't want to go to the court-house because that would mean I would never again have a reason to see her, or maybe I just wanted to sit on a rooftop on the windiest and coldest day in Maine this year, either way, I reached for her hand, and she glanced at me when we connected. "Why don't we finish the lights first? Then we can go."

She shook her head. "It's okay. I can do it when we get back."

What turning away couldn't hide, the crack in her voice, made me feel like an ass.

"Lis, we're already up here." And it wasn't likely to get any warmer now.

She nodded. "But the lights are down there." She motioned to the lawn with her head then pointed as if I didn't get it.

"Yeah." And I chuckled because this meant she wasn't making me leave. And even if it was just a few more hours, I was still married to Felicity which meant I couldn't marry Beth. And something about that, everything about that, made me happier than I'd been since…a really long time ago.

I hadn't seen her in years, didn't know anything about her life now, but I knew the twitching of her lips meant she wasn't sure. The blank stare meant she was lost in a decision. And the shivering meant she was freezing cold.

"Look, why don't you go inside and warm up while I finish the roof?" She shook her head and shot me the go to hell look, one cocked brow, half-pursed lips. "Come on, Lis. You're cold and I'm here. Might as well make use of me. I'll hang the lights. We'll go to the courthouse. It's a win/win."

Not so much, but I wanted her to go inside and get warmed up, not stay here on the roof.

Was it pathetic that I had to convince her to put off the trip to the courthouse to dissolve a marriage I'd walked out on a decade ago? Of course, it was. But I'd always been on the wrong side of pathetic when it came to Felicity.

One Decade Ago

MY STOMACH CHURNED. I couldn't breathe. Not only had I lost any hope I ever had of becoming a doctor, but I had to tell Felicity the entire truth, a truth that guaranteed I was going to lose her *and* hurt her.

Oh *fuck*. What was this going to do to her? My skin tightened and my heart ached. I felt powerless. Angry. Guilty. I wanted to die, even though death was too good for me. More I wanted to kill Ryder. This was all his fault. Well, not all, but…fuck, man. What did we do?

Two hours ago, they told me my fate. Suspended pending an investigation. Then they'd filed out of the room. Left me alone to mourn my fate. And I was tired. So, fucking tired. Not that I had anywhere to go to sleep. I wasn't even allowed to go back to the frat house except to pick up some stuff until the investigation, which was not going to land in my favor, was finished.

And for what? Because…I was an idiot and went along with Ryder. Because I didn't stand up for myself. Because I didn't think he would put it online. But I should've known. This was my responsibility. I knew about the cameras. I knew the boat was wired and that those wires live-streamed back to the computer in his room at the frat house. I just didn't think he would ever...do this. To the pledges maybe. But not to us, to his friends.

I should've known, and damn, wouldn't that have just been a fitting title for my memoir, I should've known.

But I couldn't sit in this room any longer. I didn't need to see the shelves of books, or the canvas rendering of the Glouster shield with its motto of *Loyalty, Honesty and Courage* on a banner at the bottom. Or my reflection in the shiny polished table, I had to get out of there.

I walked out. I even thought about just never stopping, most especially when I passed Felicity, and she turned to catch up with me. "Hey, you."

I couldn't talk, not without falling apart in front of her, so I nodded, faced the front, and kept walking until she tugged on my sleeve.

"Where's the fire, Finn? Slow down, my legs are shorter."

Right now, I couldn't look at her. I couldn't speak. Couldn't do more than hold her against me, crushed her was probably more accurate. Not that I wanted to hurt her, but I wanted to savor every touch for as long as I could, and maybe if I held her tight enough, she wouldn't go away. When she squeezed me and held on, my heart broke more.

"Finn? You're scaring me." But she didn't let go. Even when I couldn't hold back a sob. "Finn...," Her phone vibrated in her pocket. Three times quickly. Shit. I had to do this now before someone else got to her. There wasn't time left to treasure the way she felt in my arms. No time to figure out how to say it. If I didn't tell her and she found out from someone else, there wouldn't be any coming back from it.

My stomach ached as she pulled out her cell.

I took it before she could read the message that lit up across the top of her screen. "Me first, okay?"

She nodded and let me lead her to a bench on the lawn. "You are really scaring me, Finn."

And it was only going to get worse. When she sat beside me, I turned to face her, took her hands in mine, and swallowed back the lump of tears in my throat. But I couldn't make it work. I held back the tears but the sound that squeaked out of my throat wasn't a happy sound. "No fucking around, Lis. It's so bad."

"What? Tell me. It's okay, whatever it is. We'll work it out or get through it or...whatever." She cupped my face with her palm, and I closed my eyes even though that made me feel like an even bigger asshole and we were out in the open, where anyone could see. She lowered her voice to a whisper and leaned her forehead against mine. "It's okay. I love you no matter what."

And if ever there was a time we were going to test that theory it was now.

"There's a video of us together." My voice was weak. The voice of a pussy. I cleared my throat and tried again. "Ryder uploaded it, yours and a couple others. He was charging money..."

I shook my head because it was disgusting. "I'm so sorry, Lis."

The pain and regret in my voice were real. Mine.

But she chuckled and held me for a minute. "Worst

case, my dad finds out and…" She shook her head. "Whatever. It's not that big a deal."

But some of the light in her eyes faded. "Honestly. Who cares about some college sex video? Probably three people have seen it."

It was more, but the situation was untenable. The word viral wasn't likely to help. Cowardly or not, I nodded again.

Then she pulled me onto my feet and held my hand in hers. "Come on."

"Lis…" I needed to get this over with. Finish it now so I could figure out what to do. She dragged me a few yards before I dug in and we stopped.

"What are you doing?" This was the path to the library. I wasn't even sure if I was allowed to go in there. "Where are we going?"

"I want to look it up. I want to see it." Turned out that it was also the path to her apartment across campus, the one she shared with Sofia. When we walked in, I took a moment to be thankful Sofia wasn't there. If she knew, she would have plenty to say. And if this was my last night with Felicity, because I had to tell her the rest before this night went further, then I didn't want to spend it fighting with her best friend.

I sat beside her on the bed as she pulled out her laptop. "Okay. What do I Google?"

I reached to close the lid to the computer, but she held it open.

"This is serious, Lis." My eyes went watery, and I blew out a slow breath. "I didn't know he was going to upload."

"It's okay." She ran a hand over my forearm and gave a

weak squeeze when she got to my wrist. But then the video account appeared. "93,415 hits?"

She closed the screen. "Oh, shit."

"I'm so sorry, Lis. So sorry." I couldn't even look at her. Knowing I was going to lose her hurt too bad.

"So, you said." And she sniffed and wiped her eyes. "But you knew he was filming us?"

I couldn't lie. This was her life too and she deserved the truth. "Yeah."

Even if it made me look like a dick. Which I'd always been good at hiding before. But I didn't want to be that guy anymore. Not with her. "Lis…"

It took her a long time to look away from me, to stop hating me with her eyes. When she went back to typing before she looked up again, and her voice was lower, sadder, we both knew the answer to her question, and it wasn't one that helped my case. "Did the other girls know?"

I shook my head. "No."

Then it went back to being silent. For a minute.

"Is it wrong that I still want to see it?" Her skin went dark with color. "Just the one…I'm in. You know. I'm…curious."

My guts twisted. "I got to go."

She shot me a quick glare that turned into a pleading gaze. "Look. You did something wrong. Stupid. Asinine. Totally slutty."

She shook her head, not accepting my cowardice. "You just have to apologize and mean it. Fix what you can and move on."

She pulled in a slow breath then let it out slower. "It's not like you can undo it."

She was so wise. So wonderful. "How do I fix it?"

"I don't know." She sat back when I didn't look away. "Hey, don't blame me. I'm not the one who Kardashian-ed my way onto the internet."

She shrugged. "Not on purpose anyway." I hung my head, and she nudged me with her shoulder. "Oh, come on. Couple years, you'll either be a break-out porn star or this will have all blown over before you get your own 'Keeping up' reality show. But this isn't the worst thing."

Fuck me. I had to tell her. She didn't know, but if I lost her now…, "I'm probably getting kicked out of the university."

She shrugged. "There are other schools."

"None that'll take me after this gets out." My head was about to explode. I had nowhere to go, no future, and every fucking bit of it was my own fault. "I'm going to end up a shift manager at the Taco Hut. Old and alone in my parents' basement. Spend my best years jerking off to old *Playboys* Dad keeps in the closet downstairs."

I wasn't making light of it. If I ended up broke, old, and alone, I deserved it.

But she smiled and for a minute, my worries disappeared.

"No way you're getting shift manager." She ran her hand over my cheek. "Finn, you did some dumb shit. You can't undo it, so what are you going to do about it?"

With her arms folded under her breasts and the grim

look on her face, it wasn't rocket science to know I would be doing it without her.

And it broke me. Crumbled my courage. "I'm so sorry." The shame flooded me and for now, because I was losing every fucking thing I ever cared about, I let the tears fall. Let my shoulders shake and my breaths come in patchy huffs. Or maybe these things happened, and I was powerless to stop them. Like I was powerless about everything else.

She pulled me close. "Come on. If you're going to ugly cry on me, let's lie down."

Something about her behavior was off. She should have been throwing things at me. At the very least, she should've been cursing. Instead, she smoothed my hair, laid her head on my chest, and hugged me.

And I sat up. "Lis…did you know?"

Her sigh was all the confirmation I needed. "Kind of. My dad's the chancellor. Of course, I didn't expect to see my own hoo-ha on the screen but…"

She brushed her hair behind her ear.

"He told me about the boat and that they were talking to the Alphas today. Your name came up. Then my name came up." She puffed up her cheeks, widened her eyes, and exhaled. "Yeah. That was awkward."

"But you knew and that's why you aren't mad." Now it all made sense. She'd been able to prepare herself.

"Oh, I'm mad." She put her head back on my shoulder, and I held her because I didn't know how much longer I'd be able to. "I just think you've had a bad enough day without fighting with me on top of it. So, I'm…pacing myself. Saving some good stuff for tomorrow."

After a minute, she pulled away, hard, and sat up. I moved beside her.

"But there's one thing I have to know now." There was a short pause and I nodded. "Seriously, Finn. Why would you do this?"

I had no answer. No clue. "I don't know."

She shook her head. "*I don't know.* Come on now, Finn. That's not good enough. You videoed me, us together. And let your friend put it online."

She closed her eyes, hung her head, and laid her hand over her chest. "And my dad's going to see it because the authorities, and the school's senior staff, has to go through and figure out who the girls are so they can be contacted. He has to tell them so that they can press charges against you if they want."

She sniffed and her eyes pooled with tears. "Did you know he was making those videos? Of us? Of you?"

"Kind of." The story was way bigger than what she knew. Way bigger than I could tell her. "I knew he was making videos but not of us. Not of me or Keaton or Jameson. Sometimes, he would make the younger guys, the pledges, take a girl to the boat and…the video would stream at the house. We'd rate them on their…it was stupid, okay? And I wish…" Oh fuck, did I wish. "But I didn't know he was…that we were…or that he'd put them online."

"So, your friends were… watching…rating…fuck." She hiccupped and cried some more. And for about ten minutes, she sobbed her heart out, trembled, sniffed, then stopped like she'd flipped a switch. Toughest chick I'd ever met. "Okay, so I was just thinking of all the reasons to break up with you."

I knew it, but how did I stop it? I could deal with anything, even this shit, anything but losing her. "And?"

"And I've decided, I love you too much." She shook her head. "And don't you dare act smug right now because I just don't think I could take that. So, no smiling. No gloating that I love you too much to hate you."

But she was wrong. I wasn't smug. I was grateful. Determined to make this up to her. No matter what it took.

"Whatever you did with anyone else, I can't help you with, but...my dad said you could end up...in trouble with the law." Yeah. They'd told me that, too. "But if we're married, they can't make me testify against you."

She chuckled. "So, what do you say? I know it's not the most romantic proposal, but Finn Makenzie, will you be my husband?"

If that was her plan to save me, I was more than willing. "Lis..."

But married. To her. It wouldn't solve the problem with school...or with anything else, but I'd have Felicity. And nothing meant more to me than that. "Yes."

6

Felicity

e weren't holding hands. We weren't even brushing shoulders. But I couldn't have been more aware of Finn's presence had I been riding on his back. Or his front.

I was aware of him. Definitely. Hyper aware. Stupid aware and trying to walk with such…awareness was apparently more difficult than I could manage gracefully. Instead, I stumbled over imaginary cracks in the sidewalk. Tripped over my perfectly tied and nearer my calves than my feet shoelaces.

"Are you happy, Lis?" His voice rasped, husky and rugged. Serious.

As if walking next to him wasn't enough to throw me off balance, random, out-of-the-blue questions would do it. I staggered a step, caught myself, and managed to look up at him without face-planting on the sidewalk. "Define happy."

"You know…dance in the rain, have a snowball fight, laugh until you pee happy. Are you?"

Since my answer made me sound like a candidate for Prozac, I smiled at him. "Are you?"

"I have my moments." He smiled, and for a second, I wondered if he was thinking about another woman. But since that did nothing to make me walk straighter or be *happier,* I ignored what he could have been thinking about in favor of what *we* needed to be thinking about. "I'm pretty happy right now."

"Good." I cleared my throat. What the hell was I supposed to do with *happy right now*? What the hell was that supposed to mean. Happy to be getting a divorce? Happy to be engaged to someone else? Or happy to be here with me? I shoved the dangerous thought to the side. "So the divorce shouldn't take long. Marty," the only attorney I knew and certainly the only one willing to draw up papers at 6 o'clock in the morning on the Monday before Christmas, "said once we sign, we can go before the judge, and he'll explain what happened to the other papers. Then as soon as the judge signs off, probably Wednesday if we can get on the docket, then you'll be all free to get married."

Those words tasted bitter. Or maybe it wasn't the words themselves, but the picture they inspired. Finn waiting at the end of an aisle, smiling as some nameless, faceless woman walked toward him.

"Oh, okay." He frowned. "That's good."

He nodded and watched his feet as we walked toward Marty's office for our appointment. Not the one we'd missed to hang the lights, but one Marty had grumbled would keep him from a meatloaf dinner at his mom's. I owed him big for that one.

We walked past the square where the Christmas festival was gearing up for tonight's festivities. The week before Christmas was always a big deal in Glouster. And tonight, we had a snowman-making contest with fake snow, caroling on the square, and hot cinnamon apple cider while Mrs. Oberneuf led the Glouster ballet troop's version of the Nutcracker. And every night, Joe Langdon offered carriage rides that zipped through town for the Christmas light tour. Hence the reason I had to risk life and limb to frostbite to hang lights.

There were a thousand things I wanted to know about Finn. What happened after he left? Where had he ended up? If he made it to medical school after all? Why he left me? But in lieu of saying anything with substance, I smiled up at him. "You'll like Marty. He isn't a typical lawyer."

And by typical, I meant in any way normal. He was silver-spoon born and gold-plated bred. So, he never charged for legal services, he just expected to be repaid with a good deed. Which meant, since he was chairman of all things Christmas festival, I had to play one of the elves to his Santa for this week's festivities, but I didn't mind. Handing out gifts and taking pictures was a small price to pay. Especially since I did it every year anyway.

"I'm sure he'll be fine."

If fine meant a Colonel Sanders/Santa Clause look-alike, mustache and beard trimmed according to time of year, with a law degree and an over-abundance of year-round cheer, then yeah. He'd be fine.

For just a minute, walking beside Finn, I could see us doing this every year, being together, celebrating. Walking under the awnings down main street and caroling with the church choir. But then the fantasy disappeared. "So, tell me about your fiancée."

Nothing like being my own wet blanket.

He shrugged. "It's complicated."

Not the ringing endorsement of love, the list of her positive traits that I expected. "Complicated. That's a big word for someone who's supposed to be the love of your life."

He didn't look at me. Didn't touch me. Almost didn't speak loud enough so that I could hear. "I already had my shot at that."

There was a pause while we both let that sink in. "Anyway, you might know her. She went to school here, to the university with us." His voice dropped to that low timbre, the one that made my toes curl and my eyes close as if I could capture the sound and keep it.

Fortunately, I opened my eyes before I ran into Mrs. Chester, who was in charge of sprinkling the fake snow at the edges of the sidewalks until the real snow came. Couldn't have a picturesque Christmas town without snow, and the bed and breakfasts in Maine needed the tourist business. In summer, we had the ocean, but winter was windy and cold, so they capitalized where they could.

"Did you finally go out and get you one of those internet boyfriends? I hope you didn't overpay. Some of those online gigolos demand such a big going price." She snickered and covered her mouth. "Maybe I should call it a big *coming* price."

Mrs. Chester gave Finn an up-and-down appraisal that lingered in all his best spots. "She's been alone too long. And you look like you know your way around a woman." She glanced at me and nodded. "Probably worth the up-charge."

Finn smiled and ducked his head, his skin, for such a confident guy once upon a time, went pink. But Mrs. Chester wasn't quite done yet. "And if there's anyone who needs her block blown out, it's Felicity."

Block blown out? *Coming price?* My mouth fell open and my skin went hot. Was she serious?

Finn, on the other hand, threw his arm around me and grinned then brushed his lips along my ear to whisper. "I could go for a stroll around your block."

Warmth spread from my cheeks straight south. Settled somewhere just below my belly button. I should've been used to it since I'd never quite developed an immunity to Finn and how he made me feel. But I would've thought all that emotion would have faded in a decade. What did it make me that just a look or a word from this guy could make me wet and desperate? That I was still weak for a guy who almost destroyed me?

I stared at Mrs. Chester. "My block is just fine, and Finn's only going to be here a couple days."

Mrs. Chester laughed again. "I didn't say you had to marry him. Internet boys are all about pleasure. Getting in and getting out."

For being old enough to be my mom's mom, Mrs. Chester seemed to have information of the illicit and modern kind. And I was by no means a prude. Never really met an inhibition I couldn't work my way around, but I wasn't a civil war survivor either. And I didn't often stop on the street to spew my uninhibited advice to the towns-folk either. Of course, I wasn't Mrs. Chester.

I had to silently remind myself that Finn belonged to someone else. He had a fiancée. Loved another woman enough to marry her. A better person than me wouldn't have stood on that sidewalk debating with herself whether or not one night with me would ruin Finn's new marriage if we stuck to the one-night theory and made it an abso-lute, and never saw each other again. Maybe if we didn't get loud enough to shatter windows and alert the neigh-bors of our illicit activities nobody would know anyway. I almost had myself convinced we could make it work until that last one. Sex with Finn was...amazing, an earth-moving experience. Loud anyway and...did I mention amazing? Because it was.

"He's getting married, Mrs. C. To someone else." I wanted to spit to get the taste of that mess of syllables out of my mouth.

Instead, I quietly stared at Mrs. Chester and felt her frown all the way to my soul. I'd battled the same senti-ment all morning. "That's a shame." She patted my hand as if I'd suffered a tragedy then she pulled me in for a hug. "Maybe he has a friend?"

She paused for a second. "Or maybe the fiancée never has to know? You could use my place. I'm never there. You could use some of your woman skills and lure him." What she'd thought was a whisper, wasn't even close, and Finn chuckled then covered it by pretending to wipe the lower section of his mouth. And…shameful as it was, I was glad she'd said the words aloud. Planted a seed in his head. Then I hated myself for it.

I pulled away from Mrs. C. and glanced at Finn. "He was in love enough to propose. I wouldn't even *try* to lure him." He frowned, looked away, and didn't affirm my goodness and purity for not using my wiles to tempt him. When he glanced back, our gazes locked, and my passion smoldered as I imagined his doing the same.

It took a moment to come back to my senses, to wipe away the image of him kissing his way down my body, of kissing my way down his. But somehow, I'd ended up in front of him with my hand slipping over his chest, across a button on his shirt, and I shook off the lust and yanked away.

Instead of hauling me against him for a kiss that said his fiancée didn't matter to him, what was supposed to happen, he cleared his throat and took a step back. "We should go."

I nodded because words failed.

"It was nice to see you." Finn gave her a little wave then walked a couple steps. When I didn't immediately follow, he stopped and turned, widened his eyes, and gave me a little wave. When we were out of earshot, he stopped walking, so I did too.

"What?"

"You have a history with internet boys?"

Mrs. C hadn't said anything that should've made him think I did. "Not that anything I do is your business, but no." He stared long enough I ran a cautionary hand under my nose then sighed. There was no reason for me to humiliate myself with honesty, to put all my business out there between us, but what brain and mouth each knew were different. Apparently. "I haven't had a relationship since you packed up and left me. I dated a little, but nothing ever stuck."

His mouth twitched, and I wanted to punch him. Complicated or not, he had a future in front of him with someone he obviously loved. I had the new prospect of internet dating to look forward to.

Oh yeah. I would be punching him at the next available opportunity.

"I'm sorry." He looked into my eyes and my heart clenched at the great return of all my loving feelings as if it was trying to protect me.

Thankfully, where my heart failed, my legs took up the cause and carried me toward the courthouse. The last thing I needed was to spurt my feelings for Finn all over the town square.

When he caught up, I didn't stop walking but there was something we needed to get straight now that my brain had my feelings for him in a chokehold. "I don't need your pity, Finn. I'm happy with my life."

And I'd honed my lying skills so much that even I almost believed me. "I have a great job. Some money saved." A lot of money, actually.

"I can pick up and go whenever I want." Not that I ever did. "So, I don't need your pity."

Saying it a second time made it real. Right?

One Decade Ago

THE CLICKETY-CLACK of her heels on the concrete kept me well-appraised of her proximity, just in case the volume she called out to me didn't. "Felicity! Felicity Fields! Wait!"

No one on campus willingly stopped for Beth Cooper, the same woman who wore her press pass like jewelry or some sort of all-access badge. It was almost a given that any conversation with her would end up in print or on some digital forum. Not because she was gossipy but because Beth Cooper didn't have conversations that weren't purposeful to benefitting her career or her next great story.

And thanks to the Alpha Alpha Phi scandal unfolding right under her nose, she was all over the front pages. She wrote a story picked up by the AP and printed in more newspapers than the Glouster Messenger. Digitally, she'd gone viral. But now that the school was national news, she had to get the story before someone else found something bigger.

Hence the chasing. "Felicity Fields! Stop!"

She had the voice of a screeching falcon, loud and high-pitched.

Because she wasn't known for giving up, and I had no

intention of telling her anything anyway, I stopped. Waited for her to catch up and then catch her breath.

She stared hard at me as if she was trying to gauge the details she would use in her article. Maybe my hair color. How I dressed. My connection to the university's administration. With Beth Cooper, there was no telling. But there was also no way I was willingly giving her anything to use. "I don't have a comment, Beth."

"We'll see." Her smug smile said this was not going to be much fun for me. She shuffled books in her left arm to her right then used her free hand to root through a bag slung over her shoulder. After a couple of seconds during which I considered walking off, she pulled out a small notebook, leather-bound, black, long, and slender, the kind cops used in all the best TV dramas. "Do you know Finn Makenzie?"

It was chilly outside. Fall had arrived, spent a day, then left leaving winter to take over. I blew into my closed fist to warm my fingers then rubbed my palms together and started walking again. She fell into step beside me.

Her first question wasn't quite a firebomb but not something I planned to answer either. "You're going to have to do better than that."

I didn't say anything, just kept right on walking. That didn't deter her, however. Oh no, not Little Miss Junior Reporter with her nose in everyone's business.

"Did you know he was making videos? That they planned to put them online and charge money...," She took a long pause which said to me that she wasn't just a reporter but might've had a more personal connection. A victim's connection. "For people to look at them?"

I knew now. That counted. I wasn't going to tell her that, because I wasn't going to tell her anything. I blinked at her slowly, as if she was very stupid and needed time to catch my point. Which she did.

"Okay." She whistled a breath in through her nose and let it out through her lips. "Did you know you're not the only one Finn used as a co-star?"

I wasn't naïve enough to think he'd only "been with" me. Nor was I dumb enough to think I was the only one he filmed. But I had to focus on breathing now because it didn't take a genius to know she was ramping up.

"Two years this has been going on. That's a lot of girls." She waved the paper at me again.

I could've lived without the teeth clenching and the heat of her stare burning my skin.

"Do you care about the other girls? Their humiliation?" She grabbed my sleeve and we both stopped walking. "They're all giving statements to me, to the police. They want these bastards exposed. This is only going to get bigger."

Breathe, I reminded myself.

"More details are going in the paper every day. I know you probably think you're in love with him and he's in love with you, but this is what he does. He's charming and beautiful. They all are and it's hard to believe someone like him would do this, right?" If I hadn't been certain before, I knew now. Beth Cooper was one of Finn's...co-stars. She hardened her voice and stared through me. "It's only a matter of time until the number of girls on this list goes up, the details come out, and Finn gets charged."

Charged. With a crime. Shit.

"Felicity. They did a horrible thing to you. To these women." She held up her list and lowered her voice, probably thinking she could use kinship or my empathy to make me talk to her. But she didn't have to tell me how bad it was. I knew.

I leaned into her close and I saw her eyes grow big, eager for the juicy details. I paused, took a deep breath as if about to let it all out, and said four short words. I looked dead into her eyes with a steely gaze of my own.

"I have no comment."

And I meant it. Especially when all I really wanted was to find Finn and see if we could figure out a way to work through this without him having to go to jail.

She sighed. "I hope you're not one of those girls who's blaming the victims."

Which, in her opinion, no matter what I thought, I was one of those victims, so that was crazy. "Finn Makenzie and Ryder Kennedy, Jameson King and Keaton Shaw."

As if she thought I didn't know of or about the others, she nodded. "Yeah. Those are the other guys going down for this. Those are the names that people are going to remember. We trusted them. And this is our chance to spin the story the way we want it. To tell everyone we were victimized and maybe we can use our experience to help someone else. Someone who doesn't have a voice."

Her points were valid, but it was Finn, and my loyalties were divided between what I knew was expected of me as a victim and what I felt not just about Finn, but about what happened. So, I reiterated my point.

"I have no comment." It was the only safe thing to say. The only thing no one could twist. "And I have to go."

I turned to walk away, but her words stuck with me. How could I marry Finn knowing what he'd done? How could I not use my voice to tell the world this was wrong?

7

Finn

 ’d never met the man responsible for my first attempt at divorce from Felicity until now. He was taller than I imagined. But the horn-rimmed glasses were right on. And the puny frame. Along with the way he blushed and smiled, choked on his tongue whenever Felicity spoke to him.

But I could be a good sport because he'd only been doing his job. I held out my hand. "Marty."

Felicity chuckled. "That isn't Marty. Finn, this is Dakota, Marty's office assistant." Instead of shaking his hand, she pulled him down for a hug. A hug for fuck's sake. Like they were tight. Like he'd seen her naked. And I hated him. Unreasonable, but honest.

I curled my fingers, ready to pounce because if the hand at the small of her back moved so much as one millimeter lower, secretary boy was going to eat at least the four front teeth in his goofy-looking face.

When she pulled back, she took a look at me, then moved a step closer to *Dakota*. She frowned. "What's wrong?"

"Wrong? Why would something be wrong?" Not only had I taken up speed talking, but I went from bass to soprano.

"Because you look like you ate glass and you sound like I'm squeezing your…" She glanced at my crotch. "You know, balls."

And now, with her talking about anything ball-related, I had an entirely different problem. "I'm fine."

Fine for a guy who was busy trying to name all the states and capitals in his head rather than concentrating on her smile, or the hand *Dakota* still had resting on her back.

"Okay." She smiled and looked up at the soon-to-be-without-a-left-hand jackass still touching her. "Is Marty in?"

Dakota, I couldn't even think his name without mimicking how Felicity said it, shook his head.

"His daughter went into labor this morning and he said to tell you he needed to reschedule for next week." He looked at me, still smiling, then frowned, pulled his head back, and turned toward Felicity. "It's his first grandbaby. They're very excited."

"I can't wait for a week. I'm getting married on Saturday." The words burned a path from my gut up to my throat and out of my mouth, but since I didn't have a choice, I had to get this straightened out. Felicity blew out a breath, loud, through a little O made by her pursed lips. "I mean, is there anyone else we can see?"

Dakota looked at me. "Sh-sure. But you'll have to drive over and see Dan Schilling in Kennebunkport. He's the guy who used to date Susie Biggelo. You remember?"

He cocked an eyebrow at Felicity. She shook her head, and he shrugged. No big deal?

"Or there's a guy in York or—or—or," he pointed and waved his hand, excited and louder, "you know that one, the one in Gorham that Marty likes. But there's a storm blowing in."

His tongue clicked against his teeth and he narrowed one eye into a Popeye the Sailor face. "So, you might be better to wait to go anywhere until tomorrow."

Oh great. Now he was a travel agent. And a weatherman.

But I didn't care so much about Dakota when I looked at Felicity, who'd pulled her lip between her teeth and cast her eyes down. "A storm, huh?"

She didn't look at me, but the quiver in her chin said all the words.

Not that I knew what they meant or why the prospect of a storm keeping her from divorcing me when she hadn't even known she was still married to me would be enough to make her cry, but a tear slipped down her cheek. "Hey. You okay, Lis?"

She sniffed, shook her head, wiped her eyes, and held up her hand. "I'm fine."

Dakota moved in and he was the only one who didn't seem to know he was a couple seconds from losing the arm he clearly planned to slip around Felicity's waist. I watched, waiting while he decided what to do. He pulled the arm back to his side.

And it wasn't fair. I knew it. She had every right to be with…him. Jealousy wasn't a look I wanted her to see on me. And I wanted her to be happy.

Bullshit.

I wanted her to be with me. But since Beth was making sure me being with Felicity wasn't an option, I couldn't stand in the way of her finding someone else or being with someone else she'd already found. Dammit.

But like the man I should've been to keep her, I smiled and nodded to the door. "I'm going to wait outside. Give you guys a minute."

"What?" Her mouth dropped open and her eyes narrowed. "What the hell are you talking about?"

I didn't answer because Dakota laughed. "I think he thinks we're together."

He shook his head and grinned, holding his left hand up so I could see the gold band on his third finger. "I'm married to Sofia."

Sofia. I would've never guessed. "Oh, wow. Congratulations."

He was definitely tougher than I thought then.

"Five years ago." Felicity crossed her arms and stared at me, shaking her head.

Dakota laughed. "Wait until I tell Sofia you thought…"

He didn't get to finish because Felicity stepped closer to me. "Were you jealous?"

"No." Too fast. Too loud. Too much. And no one in that

room believed me. I certainly didn't. Dakota's wide eyes and smirk and the slight tilt to Lis's head and the way she chewed the corner of her lower lip said I might as well have saved my indignation.

She looked at him, and they both looked at me. I'd spent the last ten years on the straight and narrow. I hadn't told so much as a teeny tiny fib because I took my second chance seriously. And maybe that was why I was a shitty liar.

"We should go." I motioned to the door with my head.

Felicity smiled then glanced at Dakota who also smiled. I waited outside because I needed a minute. The relief at knowing she wasn't with Dakota was as powerful as any other emotion I'd ever had.

After a few minutes, where I adjusted my scarf, pulled on a pair of gloves, yanked a stocking cap out of my pocket and put it on, and decided I would rather sweat to death than freeze, she finally made it out the door.

"I called Dan Schilling and made an appointment for tomorrow." After that, she walked beside me silently for the first block. "You never did get to tell me about your fiancée. I mean, you said it was complicated and that she went to Glouster, but..." She shrugged. "I want to hear the great love story."

Well, she wouldn't hear that about me and Beth. No matter how I dressed it up.

"Not much else to tell, I guess." The last thing I wanted to talk about was my impending wedding to Beth. "She made me an offer I couldn't refuse."

Not if I wanted to shield Lis and somehow maintain my reputation.

"She asked you?" When I nodded, Felicity chuckled, but if sound had edges, this one would've been all points and sharp lines.

"Yeah." Not asked as much as demanded. More information I would keep to myself because it wouldn't do any good to say it out loud.

"And you said yes." This wasn't a question I needed to answer because it wasn't a question. It was Felicity just saying the words and more to herself than to me. This time her laugh was softer, a sweeter sound than I remembered. Whether it was age or the fading of my memories, everything about Felicity was better now than before. "I guess I always just hoped that wherever you were or whatever you were doing, you'd still be thinking of me and...I don't know."

She shook her head.

"Longing, maybe. I guess I'm just a little sad that you didn't wait..." She paused, even stopped walking and rolled her eyes. "An entire decade. Pretty silly, huh?"

We started walking again because I couldn't, didn't want to tell her I'd waited. It wouldn't be fair to either of us to tell her no other woman measured up to her. That the eleven days I spent as her husband were the best days of my life and carried me through some long, lonely years. Not that I'd been alone all that time, but aside from a few one-night stands, and a couple of friends with benefits, nothing ever stuck.

"Not silly at all."

She cleared her throat and shoved her hands into her pockets. "Does your...fiancée know you're staying with me?"

I didn't miss the pause or the squeak in her tone when she said the word *fiancée*. The question was reasonable, but I didn't like having to answer it. I didn't like Felicity thinking anyone had power over me. Because in truth, the only one who had the power to keep me from making my own decisions was her. Felicity Lorelei Fields Makenzie. The only woman I would die to protect. And by die, I meant marry Beth Cooper.

"No, but she wouldn't care. We don't have that kind of relationship." And wasn't that the saddest thing I'd ever said? I might have been a guy in the minority, but I wanted a woman who *needed* to know where I was, who cared about who I spent time with when I wasn't with her, who didn't mind that I needed and cared in the same ways.

In our blissful eleven days of marriage, I'd never noticed that Felicity was a tongue-clucker. Apparently, she was because she did. "I would care."

She stopped walking again and this time moved in front of me.

"You wouldn't trust me?" I couldn't blame her. I wasn't entirely sure I was in a situation where I could be trusted.

She slid her hands up my chest, over my coat but I felt the touch like it was her palm against my bare skin. Everything burned.

"No, that's not what I'm saying." Her gaze caught mine, held, and I didn't want to move. Ever. Again. "I wouldn't trust me."

Her tongue swiped her lower lip before it disappeared into her mouth. Her eyelids fluttered. Her fingers curled into the fabric of my coat. I wanted to stay this way for the rest of my life.

The fact of the matter was that we were standing in the freezing cold Maine winds on a public street with our arms wrapped around each other, and I was engaged to someone else. And even though it was the very last thing I wanted to do, I pulled my arms back and took a step away.

"We should get out of this wind." If there was a more chickenshit way out of this, I was certain to find it, but for now, this had to do.

She nodded, and we started walking.

How I'd let myself get talked into leaving her or signing those divorce papers or becoming engaged to someone else when all I wanted in the world was Felicity would always be one of those mysteries for me that I would never figure out how to solve.

One Decade Ago

FELICITY BUSTED through the bathroom door, red-faced, and out of breath. Beautiful and sexy, also about three minutes too late to join me in the shower. "I don't want you to go to jail."

To this point, even though we all knew it was a possibility, no one had mentioned the j-word. We hadn't talked prison cells or striped jumpsuits, flip-flops for shoes, or no touching on visiting days. Although I'd thought a lot about it. Especially since we'd all, Jameson, Keaton, Ryder and I, been called to the police station, all given statements, all been kicked off the team and suspended from school pending investigation, but no one had said *jail* until now, and I certainly didn't expect it to be her.

Completely naked, hair still dripping, body mostly dried, I wrapped a towel around my waist and crossed my arms. "I don't want to go to jail."

She still had her coat on, but she walked in, put her forehead against my chest, and tucked her freezing cold hands between my wrists and my sternum. I inhaled a sharp breath then folded my arms around her, trying to soothe her because it was what we both needed, but my body always responded to having her so close and my towel didn't leave much room to hide. Still, I held her.

After a few minutes, she lifted her head and looked into my eyes as her teeth worked her bottom lip. "I'm going to talk to my dad."

I'd dragged her into this enough as it was. Even though, honestly, I didn't mean to. There was a video out there of us together and it had been edited to make her look like she was the aggressor in our interlude. And there were snippets and four-second pieces of her asking me to do things nobody ever wanted to say publicly. If she was my kid, the last thing I would have wanted to do was help the bastard who let her be humiliated like that. I didn't expect the chancellor of the university, who hadn't even been able to look at me as he told me I was suspended, to be different.

"No, Lis. I could never ask your dad to help me."

She stepped back and leaned against the wall, her pose mirroring mine against the vanity. "You're not asking. I am."

Then, as if the discussion was closed, she walked out of the bathroom, hers because I'd been staying in the apartment she shared with Sofia since I got kicked out of the Alpha house. It smelled better, the furniture matched, and I spent every night with the most wonderful girl I'd ever met. If I had to get kicked out of the frat house, this wasn't a bad alternative living space. Not at all.

After I pulled on my clothes, I walked into her room. She'd shucked the coat, kicked off her boots, and tossed her bag onto the bed. "You want to tell me what happened?"

The mattress dipped when I sat beside her, and I brought her knuckles to my lips for a kiss. If there were a thousand hours in a day instead of the meager twenty-four, and I could spend them all with her, I would spend as many as I could touching and kissing her anywhere she'd let me.

"Beth freaking Cooper happened. She's…"

Probably one of the girls I slept with on video since I'd been dating her before I met Felicity and Beth and I had been together at the boat. "She's probably hurting, too."

And when Beth hurt, she liked to spread it around. Although, she wasn't the one who'd put sadness in Felicity's eyes, who'd made her step back from me, who'd given away too much.

"Did you sleep with her?" Oh fuck. I never wanted to hear the sadness in her voice ever again. Especially since the truth was not going to set us free. Damn it. The last thing I wanted was to lose Felicity, as a matter of fact, I was going to do whatever it took to keep her, except lie to her. I wouldn't do that.

Her lip quivered before I even nodded.

"Yeah."

But instead of releasing the dam and letting the tears fall, she nodded. Then stood. Then started pacing. "So that's why she's shredding you online and on blogs and in newspapers and on TV now? She's pissed off because you dumped her."

That was a very basic way of putting it. A very dismissive of my crime kind of way. She clapped her hands together, then rubbed them against each other. "I can work with that."

"It wasn't like that, Lis. It isn't." If Beth was only pissed about being dumped, part of it maybe but I doubted it was the totality of her anger, I would have moved heaven and earth to make whatever I could up to her. But Beth wasn't about the intense emotional feelings stirred by a relationship gone south. For her purposes, relationships were about function and need. Anything else was beneath her. She was all business all the time. "No. She took the break-up fine."

I hadn't given her much choice. By then I'd met Felicity and I couldn't see Beth anymore. And she hadn't given two shits. "And no matter what her personal feelings are towards me, *I did* something wrong. And whether I knew about Ryder and the internet or not, there are consequences because I knew what he was doing with the pledges. I also know how Ryder's always been. And I knew about the cameras. And I still took girls to the boat."

And for the sake of honesty, because I didn't want to keep lying to her, I added, "A lot of girls."

I laid back on the bed as the gravity of the words and my situation hit me. It was right to use the word *jail* because I deserved it. Women were hurt because of what I did. Had the girl I loved more than anything in the world cared what people thought, no way would she have been able to sit there and consider asking her dad to help me.

"Yeah. I heard." She sighed from deep in her chest. "I've been trying to think of ways to excuse this. Things I could take to Dad. Like you didn't force anyone to go to the boat with you. But, on the other hand, they had a reasonable expectation that one of their most intimate moments with a man wouldn't end up on a porn site. And then I turn around and try to excuse it by saying you didn't know. But you did know, kind of. And I try to think there's no way they didn't know about you guys and what you were doing."

She chuckled, soft, almost a whisper of sound. "But I didn't know. I just liked you. And I want to be the woman who defends other women. Who has their back when stuff like this…when a man does stupid shit."

So, this was the beginning of the end. "Do you want me to leave?"

Another sigh. A head shake. A shrug. "That's the thing. I don't. And I hate that I don't. That I should, but I don't. Somehow, though, I believe you when you say you didn't know this was happening. When you said you trusted Ryder because he's been your friend since freshman year."

She stopped pacing and moved to stand in front of me, tilted my chin up so I had to look into her eyes. "The same as I believed you when you said you love me."

After a second, she moved her hand to my cheek. "Do you love me, Finn?"

She would know if I just said the words without meaning them, so I took a second and thought about it. We'd lived in her room for a week now. Slept in the same bed and not had sex because I didn't want her to think… anything. But I never wanted to go back to sleeping without her in my arms. And I never wanted to wake up again without seeing her face on the pillow next to mine.

"I love you."

She smiled as if she thought I might not say it. So, I kissed her with all the feeling and all the emotion that belonged with the words I'd just said.

"Then let me help you because I love you too, and I want to be with you, and I don't want to have to get a body cavity check every time."

There was a joke in there somewhere but more than I wanted to make her laugh, I wanted her to know I meant what I said. I loved Felicity Fields. And nothing in my life meant more to me than the fact she loved me back.

And that was why I didn't sleep with her that night. Or the next one. Or the one after that. But on the fourth day, I went with her to the courthouse and signed my name on a line beside hers. Then followed her into the judge's chambers where we stood in front of him. I held her hands in mine and looked deep into her eyes as we each promised now and forever to be together. To cherish and love each other through sickness and health, richer and poorer, for as long as we lived.

"Mrs. Finn Makenzie." If she said it once, she said it a hundred times.

And every single time, it made me happier than the last. Honest to God, I didn't know I could ever be so happy. "I like the sound of that."

I didn't come from a place where love and marriage were things we aspired to, but more things we ran from because the examples set by those who claimed love and happiness were the opposite of what it should've looked like. But this was…different than what I'd seen growing up. This was loving Felicity.

She kissed my throat and slid her hand under my shirt as I drove. "You know what I like the sound of?"

I didn't answer because I couldn't form a thought. I didn't have enough blood left in my brain for thought to be possible.

"I like the sound you make right after you put your dick inside me." Her hand slipped lower and she squeezed my cock through my pants. "And the one right before you come."

Holy shit. I was trying to drive and keep a car on the road while my *wife* taunted and tempted me with all her sexuality. And I didn't mind saying, I was weak. Especially when she squeezed my dick again. And again. And again.

"You know what I really like?" She asked me, and I waited for an answer because when I pulled up to the stoplight, she kissed me hard and deep, passionate and wanton. Hotter than…anything I'd ever lived through. "I liked watching the video of us together."

Oh. Well, there was a surprise. "Really?"

"Oh yeah." She worked the button, then the zipper on my pants, and made contact just as I pulled the car into the driveway of the furnished house we'd rented that morning. "I'm ready for the reenactment."

It was a cute cottage we'd contracted to rent and buy. It had two bedrooms, a kitchen, a dining room, and a living room. And if I had my way, we'd be reenacting that video in every room in the house.

Unfortunately, fate and her father had other ideas.

8

Felicity

*A*t some point in my life, there would come a time when I made a conscious decision to stop humiliating myself for Finn Makenzie. But ten minutes ago when I probably would've gone down on him in the middle of the sidewalk in the business district, and he rejected me, I knew today wasn't that day. And if he stayed in town, tomorrow wasn't looking so good either.

And since there was no way to move past it without falling into a hole until I could figure out what to do about it, I pretended I hadn't just made a pass at him.

"You want some coffee or tea...maybe some..." Oh yeah. "Hot chocolate."

Back in the day, Finn's passion for all things chocolate and doused in whipped cream was almost as intense as his passion on the gridiron, in the classroom, and in the bedroom. Although, I had a feeling his addiction to hot chocolate with whipped cream, sprinkles, marshmallows, and even cinnamon might have outweighed the rest. And nobody made a glass of piping hot chocolate as well as I did. I'd spent all of high school perfecting the art at Milburn's coffee shop in York. And that I'd spent eleven of the best days of my college career learning all the best things to do with the aerosol can of Redi-Whip didn't mean I had to put any of those things into practice now. Unless… he wanted to. Not that I would bring it up…on purpose.

He nodded and followed me into the kitchen. While I whipped up a batch of chocolate sweetened by the finest syrup Hershey, Pennsylvania had to offer, Finn stood close enough that I could feel the heat from his body, and I could smell his cologne, which should've been named after him since I could never smell anyone wearing it and not think of him. He was close enough to intoxicate me. And maybe that was why…

"What if throwing our divorce papers into the fire wasn't an accident?" I shot him a sidelong glance as he leaned a hip against the counter and cocked an eyebrow. And even I didn't know where I was going with this, I'd considered it more than once today. "I mean…it was an accident in that I didn't consciously mean to burn them. I don't think…but what if…"

I stirred the chocolate in the pan. "What if my subconscious knew you'd want to get married someday and this was my…*subconscious*," one-handed double pump air quote, "way of making sure I got to see you again?"

I wanted a specific answer despite the fact he'd left me

without a word, without any explanation whatsoever. But I wanted the explanation, too. I just didn't want to ask for it, so I came up with the ridiculous subconscious theory. Mostly ridiculous.

"What if it was your subconscious?" He moved to stand behind me now. All I had to do was lean back and we would be touching.

Fucking hell. This was wrong. He had a fiancée. A woman waiting for him to resolve this divorce thing and I was…not a good person.

I twisted the knob on the stove and the flame died. Along with my hope for anything to develop between me and Finn. I looked down into the pot. The milk swirled and bubbled. Truth and insight weren't going to come from middle of the night warm milk. I could boil dairy products until dawn, and it wasn't going to make me see what I already knew in my heart.

"Then we would have to ignore it." And I hated those words more than anything in my world.

Hated more that he moved to the other side of the kitchen island. Because no matter what my words said, I wanted Finn. I wanted what we had. And I knew it was unrealistic to think all those old feelings would have survived a decade and that we were the same people so being in love would make sense. I knew those things were unlikely. Unreasonable. But this was my life, my future. And I didn't want to spend it living with less than I had with him. Didn't we owe it to ourselves to try? To at least see if there was anything left? To find out if we could make it work? To at least know if we were still compatible. Jobwise. Life wise. Love wise.

I finished his cup of hot chocolate and set it in front of him. And before I could speak, his phone rang in his pocket and he pulled it out to check the screen. His eyes closed. "I have to take this."

That was okay. I needed time to figure out what to do. I needed a plan.

And I needed not to eavesdrop on his conversation. But...

"No, we couldn't do it today." He paused, and I would've bet money on him running his hand through his hair. "It's not her fault. We have an appointment for tomorrow."

He didn't sound like a man who was happy to talk to his fiancée, and it was wrong for me to be happy about that. Not that I could control how his surly voice made my heart lighter, but in my defense, I did realize it was wrong. "I know, okay, Beth. I know the wedding is in four days and I know you spent 30,000 dollars on your dress, and I know half the free world is coming to *your* wedding, and all I have to do is stand there and say *I do*. I know, okay?"

And now he sounded downright hostile. I hoped those weren't his wedding vows. "No. I haven't slept with her."

The better question, the one *I* wanted answered right now anyway, was did he want to sleep with me? And what would I do with that information if he did? "Yeah. I know what you said. I'm not going to sleep with her."

He didn't have the soft voice of a man consoling an insecure bride. He was more in the throes of homicidal rage or at least pre-wedding panic.

And it was wrong for me to be happy about it. So, I stopped. Stopped listening. Stopped grinning. Stopped trying to plot my way back into his life. I wasn't being fair and that was all there was to it. It was probably hard for her to know he was in Maine with his ex-wife when she was wherever hoping I would cooperate, and she'd get to wear her 30,000-dollar dress to marry the man of her dreams. And it wasn't her fault he was mine first. It was time to let go.

But I didn't want to.

Fuck. This was hard. Too hard.

I walked through the kitchen to the bedroom and closed myself inside. It wasn't proximity that kept me from letting him go. And it wasn't nostalgia. It was closure. We didn't have it. And it only took me an hour alone in my room to figure that out. But when I did, I marched out into the living room, then the dining room, then the kitchen with no sign of Finn in any of the rooms. I checked the front porch, then the back patio. His rental car was still parked out front, so he hadn't gone farther than a walk.

I didn't get a chance to check the garage because the doorbell rang. I ran to answer. First, because the temperature had dropped five degrees every hour since breakfast this morning, so he was probably freezing, and second because I just wanted to see his face. Pathetic, yes. To be admitted aloud, never.

But it wasn't Finn standing on the porch. It was Dad. Dad who wasn't in the mood for pleasantries or even a hello before he burst through the door. A weird little moment of déjà vu swept in on me.

"Is it true? Is he here?" He glared down at me, his hands on hips over his long gray wool coat, a scarf hung around his neck, and a decade of rage at Finn for breaking my heart after our sex tape was released online flashed in his eyes. "Is. He. Here?"

I nodded. I didn't have to ask who he meant. The rumor mill would have already been circulating one or more versions of the story. We'd talked to Mrs. Chester which was in the same realm as putting my business on a bill-board and hanging it in the center of town. Dammit. I should've been more careful, been a better actor. Dad wasn't a fan of Finn's ten years ago, and I couldn't imagine after he'd helped me through losing him that his hatred would die. Apparently.

"Is it true that you're letting him stay here, too?" When I didn't answer with more than pursed lips that said I didn't want to answer at all, he threw his hands up and turned away only to turn back a second later. Then he walked through the house and opened all the doors, including the small pantry in the kitchen, searching. "Where is he?"

"I seem to have misplaced him." And I wasn't kidding.

"Dammit, Fliss. I'm not in the mood for your sarcasm."

There was no sarcasm to it. But if Dad wasn't in the mood for sarcasm, he wouldn't have been in the mood for honesty that sounded suspiciously like it either. "Dad, he was on the phone. I went into the other room. He must've left."

"For good?" Hope lit in his eyes.

But no point in lying. "I doubt it. We have an appointment with a divorce lawyer tomorrow. We have to get this resolved because…" I shook my head. This was not my best day. Not my best life. "Because his fiancée spent a boatload on a dress, and she's very anxious for their Christmas Eve wedding."

Dad stared at me for a second before he nodded. "Are you okay?"

And this was why I'd never missed having a mom. He knew exactly what to say. What to do. How to be a friend when I needed one and a dad when I needed one of those.

"Yeah." Plus, he could spot a lie at eighty paces and knew exactly when I needed a hug.

He pulled me close and ran his hand over my hair. He smelled like pipe smoke even though he'd never touched tobacco in his life, and he felt safe. "Want me to kick his ass for coming back?"

And if any dad could, it was mine, with his muscled arms and barely fiftyish body.

But I shook my head. If there was one person I was comfortable telling the truth to, it was Dad. "No. I want you to kick his ass for leaving in the first place."

And wasn't that just the damned truth?

One Decade Ago

FINN PUT a plate in front of me and leaned down for a kiss. When he pulled back, he smiled, and I smiled and all was right in the world. It was my wedding day. And Finn Makenzie was my husband who knew his way around a kitchen. How much better could life get for one day?

"It isn't much, just a grilled steak," he'd stood outside and cooked. For me. I sighed probably seeing the world through my rose-colored glasses, but that was okay. The reddish tint made everything a bit more lovely. "And a baked potato. I didn't want to order pizza on our wedding night."

Damn, I loved his shy smile. And that he thought so hard about our wedding night.

A knock, more of a fist bang, against the door swallowed up my answer. "Felicity Fields! You open this damned door before I break it down!"

Dad.

Oh shit.

I probably should've told him about moving into this house and about my wedding. That I'd married one of the Glouster Four, that was what the papers were calling Finn and the other Alphas involved in the video scandal.

"You didn't tell your dad?"

I shook my head because I didn't feel like yelling over the banging. I stood, glanced at my steak like I was on death row and it was my last meal, then pushed Finn out of the way when I opened the door. "Daddy."

He shuffled past me and grabbed Finn by the front of the shirt, using his momentum to slam Finn into the wall. "You little son of a bitch!"

In his defense, Dad had been forced to tell me I was in one of the videos, that he was kicking my boyfriend off the football team and suspending him from school, and I hadn't mustered the courage to tell him I was moving or that I planned to marry the guy from my sex tape so I didn't have to testify in any court proceeding that might come up against said husband. And because…I loved him.

I tugged Dad's sleeve and pushed my body between him and Finn.

"You moved in with him! You moved out of your apartment with Sofia! And you didn't tell me any of it." He let go of Finn's shirt and turned away, his back to both of us.

"I'm sorry, Dad."

"He's going to ruin your life." His voice was low, colder than I'd ever heard. "Look what he's already done to you. To all those poor girls."

He scrubbed his hands over his face then spun and pounced on Finn again.

Finn didn't raise his hands, didn't fight back, didn't even speak. I, on the other hand, morphed into some sort of hysterical fishwife when Daddy twisted them both around and threw Finn into a stack of boxes of stuff I'd brought from Sofia's. Dishes inside the box shattered as Finn fell over them onto the floor.

This time, I jerked my dad's shoulder. "Stop it! He's my husband."

Dad straightened, looked over his shoulder at me, and walked out the door. And because I just couldn't let him go, couldn't leave this unresolved between us, because I knew I was the one who messed it all up, I ran after him.

"Dad, wait!" He'd made it as far as the sidewalk and stopped. But he didn't turn to look at me. Wind whipped between the houses and down the street, blowing my hair and chilling my skin, but I only cared about changing the look in my dad's eyes. "I'm sorry."

"Sorry? This isn't one of those things an apology fixes." He shook his head. "This is a guy who's going to break you. Sweetheart, you deserve better than a college drop-out, than someone you're going to have to drive to Wiscasset to see on visiting days."

I didn't know if what Finn did was a prison time offense or if Daddy mentioned Wiscasset for shock value, but the idea hit its mark, and I pictured Finn in an orange jumpsuit behind bars. But I didn't shudder, didn't gasp or cry. I stared at my Dad. My best friend. Who should've been supporting me?

And I should've talked to him about all of this, the video, my feelings for Finn, the wedding, but I didn't because I still couldn't look him in the eyes. I couldn't face the disappointment I knew I'd see there because of that goddamned video. While I hadn't been able to meet his gaze since the scandal broke, he hadn't looked at me either.

My stomach churned and I wanted nothing more than to throw my arms around him for a hug. I wanted to go back to the days before he found out about the videos, to a time when he called me every day and when we went to dinner every Thursday night and tailgated at football games on Saturdays.

"Dad. I love him."

"I can't watch you do this, Fliss." He threw up his hands and walked around his car. "Come with me. You can get an annulment, we'll fix all of this."

Because I'd never argued with him or given him a reason to be angry, so I'd never seen this side of him, it took every ounce of courage and energy I had to say, "No."

He nodded once then climbed in and drove away. Gone. And I stood there staring until his taillights faded and the car disappeared, until the wind blew through me and Finn came out to wrap my coat around my shoulders and guide me back inside.

I didn't think much more than I was sorry I hurt my dad. So sorry.

Finn wrapped his arm around my shoulder and guided me inside. Probably not the wedding night he wanted, certainly wasn't the one I'd dreamed about, but he held me through the night as I cried over the scene with my Dad. And when I woke up next to him, I wasn't so upset anymore.

9

Finn

Everything in the house smelled like Felicity, the sofa cushions, the towels, every molecule of air. Not that I minded. Felicity was one of my favorite scents. I needed only to figure out how to bottle it and take it with me when I left.

Which, even after only two days, I wasn't in a hurry to do. I liked waking up to hear her humming. And listening to her sing in the shower. I loved the way she talked to the birds when she threw birdseed out in the mornings. And the way she looked? Older. Better, if that was even possible. Her hair was longer. Eyes brighter but with a wisdom behind them that came from living.

"You want breakfast?" She poked her head around the kitchen wall and looked at me as I rubbed the sleep out of my eyes and wished for a cup of coffee that magically appeared on the table, if magically meant she walked it across the room and set it in front of me.

She looked down where the blanket covered my boxers. "You got a tent pole down there or are you just happy to see me?"

I chuckled. "Always happy to see you."

She jerked her gaze back to my face and waited a second after my shrug to shake her head.

"Your fiancée know you talk to other women that way?" I should've been the one embarrassed, but it was her cheeks that went red.

I wanted to tell her the truth, and I wanted her to stop reminding me of Beth and the wedding. "I don't talk to *other women* that way."

That she thought I would, speared something in my gut. "I don't see women other than you."

Felicity crossed her arms. "That's a good line. New material?"

I reached for the mug because I couldn't look at her. I didn't want her to see how her doubt affected me.

There wasn't much in my life I'd remained true to, thanks to time and history. My own bad behavior. Those things defined my lack of loyalty, but I'd been true to Felicity. It's why I was alone. And marrying Beth Cooper didn't mean I wasn't alone. It only meant I was alone with Beth Cooper beside me. But no way could I tell Felicity without admitting all those things to myself. So, I nodded.

"You know me." She didn't. Not anymore. "I like to keep things fresh."

She turned but not before I saw a flash of pain in her

eyes. And I couldn't let that go. I couldn't let her walk away thinking she was just another in a long line of women I hit on.

I threw the blanket off and followed her into the kitchen. "Lis…"

There was nothing I could say. Not while she was bent with her head in the fridge, and I couldn't take my eyes off her ass. That made me a pig, and Felicity deserved better. But damned if I was ever good enough of a man to look away.

And I didn't until she stood, arms full of breakfast items. "Scrambled okay?"

I nodded because I didn't give two shits about eggs and bacon. She was cooking for me. In the kitchen we shared. And it was hot. Almost as hot as the way her jeans hugged the curve of her hips, or the way her shirt defined the swell of her breasts. This was not the way to make a hard-on go down.

"Lis."

She didn't turn, but she stopped moving. Stopped adjusting her ingredients. Stopped pretending to be busy. "Finn."

It was wrong. And so right. I moved to stand behind her and breathed in the smell of her hair. Put a hand on her shoulder and would have turned her around to face me, so I could lower my head and taste her lips, but the back door opened, and Sofia breezed in.

I took a giant step back as she cocked an eyebrow, and Felicity whistled out the air stored in her puffed cheeks.

"Am I interrupting?"

I said, "Yes," at the same time Lis said, "No."

Sofia cocked an eyebrow and smiled at me. "Cozy."

Felicity shot her a withering look, and I smiled. "Was 'til you got here."

"And I see you've wiggled your way back into her personal space. Good job." Sofia chuckled and looked at Felicity. Her smile faded.

"Why aren't you dressed? It's Wednesday and we have a," she shot me a look then widened her eyes at Lis, "thing. Remember?"

Lis pursed her lips and wrinkled her brow.

"A thing. On Wednesday. Right." She glanced at me. "I have a thing."

I grinned. "Me, too." And I wasn't talking about an appointment.

"Yeah. We can all see your thing." Sofia narrowed her eyes and stared at my boxers. "But Felicity has an appointment."

Vague. Mysterious. Perplexing. "An appointment. Why don't I go along and after, we can get lunch then head off to see the lawyer?"

Sofia glanced at Felicity, and I watched them both. Felicity shifted, opened her mouth, closed it, tilted her head, and widened her eyes at Sofia. Sofia shrugged and remained as innocent looking as a thief caught red-handed.

"I'll drive." That was me being helpful, not nosy, not fishing for information about this mystery appointment.

"No!" Felicity shook her head. "No. I should be back in time for us to get to the lawyer." She glanced at

Sofia and pressed her lips together then flared one nostril.

Sofia nodded. "Oh yeah. Plenty of time. This is just a little two-hour bookstore thing."

Bookstore? "I love bookstores. What with all the books and the…books."

Wow, I went full-on lame ass. "I'll just come along. You won't even know I'm there."

She looked at Sofia while I watched her. I could almost see her mind spinning, trying to figure out a way to keep me from going along. "Oh, come on. I'm bored."

She didn't waver.

"One trip instead of two. Environmentally responsible." I added that last bit in, just for good measure. Sofia rolled her eyes at the flimsy straws I continued to grasp at. "After, I'll buy us all lunch."

"Damn, Felicity. Just tell him so he can stop this…whatever this is." Sofia wiggled her finger in front of me.

Lis shook her head and sighed.

"It's a book signing." She wouldn't meet my eyes as she twisted her hands and continued speaking. "I write romance novels."

"And she's really good." Sofia shot Felicity a wink. "Even without the slightest shred of romance in her life."

Felicity pfft-ed then crossed and uncrossed her arms, shook her head, and pfft-ed again. "I have plenty of romance in my life."

Sofia laughed. "Writing love scenes between Scottish lairds and regency ladies is not romance in your life."

Lis's face reddened. Then marooned. Then went downright brick colored. "I would never put a laird with a regency socialite." She shook her head. "And that isn't my only romance."

Fuck, how I wanted it to be. Selfishly.

Sofia chuckled. "So, you're finally willing to admit you named your vibrator?"

"Maybe we could talk about this later." Lis's words came deep and through gritted teeth.

I remembered a vibrator, from a very long time ago. One she'd named after me. Surely, it wasn't the same one?

Sofia straightened, sobered, and huffed out a loud breath. "Of course. You have to get dressed anyway because we have to go."

Oh, I had to go buy some books. The thought of reading Felicity's words, of reading about the worlds she created made me smile. She'd done it. She'd achieved her dream. I wanted to hug her and congratulate her with champagne. I wanted to tell her how proud I was between kisses.

Instead, I watched her walk away, and Sofia watched me.

"You know I'll kill you, right?" Sofia dead-eyed me hard.

Of course, I knew she'd want to. Whether or not she could…

"You almost broke her last time."

Sofia knew her gut punches. Mastered their delivery.

"I'm not here to hurt her." The last thing I ever wanted to do was to cause Felicity a moment of pain. It was hard enough to live with what I'd done to her all those years ago.

"Hmm." She laughed, short, sharp, and angry. "I don't think you can help it because you don't know."

She paused for a quick scoff and a head shake. "You just don't know."

"Then tell me." Doing what I'd done, leaving her, was hard enough. Hearing how it affected Felicity would probably kill me, but I deserved it. "And while you're at it, tell me how to fix it."

She nodded. "Don't sleep with her. And stop being the charming fuck who hangs her Christmas lights and tells her she looks pretty in the morning. Don't build her up to tear her down. And for the love of all things dear, go to a hotel. The last thing she needs is 24/7 of all of that." She waved her hands in front of me like I was today's next item up for bid.

"I can't. Hotels are all booked." If I didn't sound the least bit depressed about staying with Felicity, I couldn't help it.

She rolled her eyes. "You can lie to yourself all you want, Finn."

I wasn't lying to myself. I was lying to her, but she wasn't going to take a breath so I could admit it.

"But a blind guy could see through you. If they were giving rooms away for free, you'd still be right here because it's what *you* want."

"Maybe I'm not ready for this to be done." Of all people to say it to, to tell my truth to, I chose Sofia, the person most likely to shove her 400-dollar sneakers up my ass.

She crossed her arms. "And the whole world is about what Finn Makenzie wants, right? Never mind that you being here is going to set her back. Never mind that it took her years to get over you, to stop wishing you'd come home. Never mind anything but what you want. Right?"

Fuck. Of all people to get sound advice from, I would've bet money on anyone but Sofia.

I sighed. "She's lucky to have you."

She nodded.

"And unlucky to still be married to you. Because in her head, this is probably some karmic sign, the universe telling her that there's no such thing as mistakes. And you're going to have to convince her otherwise." She moved in close. "Because if you don't and she gets hurt by you again, I'll make that ass kicking you took from Ryder look like a walk in the fucking park."

Of all the things I'd chosen to forget about, the beating that started the beginning of the end shouldn't have been one. Maybe I forgot because there were so many better things to remember.

One Decade Ago

WAKING up next to Felicity made waking up one of my favorite parts of the day. Along with seeing her smile, hearing her laugh, and watching her sleep until she opened her eyes to look at me. In the day and a half since the wedding, we hadn't managed to do more than sleep. Too many emotions over her dad. Too much conflict.

But now, she was smiling. At me. Wearing my t-shirt after a shower that'd left her hair dripping down her back and her skin scrubbed fresh and pink. Fuck. So pretty. Beautiful. Mine.

And I was hers. Every time I thought about it, about us and our future, warmth spread through me. The rest of our lives played out in front of me. The house we would make our own, bright colors for paint, and art she drew, my hand-carved chess set, a shelf for the books we both loved, babies with her eyes and her smile, her easy-going attitude, her kindness. I wanted to give her everything, be enough for her, undo…

"Hey." She sat beside me on the bed, and I sat up so I could look at her, touch her, kiss her. When we parted, I leaned my forehead against hers, and she ran her finger down the side of my throat, soft, slow, tempting. "You could've joined me."

I grinned because I liked it when she smiled at me with those big eyes flashing her happiness. They made her special brand of sexiness all the sexier. I hadn't tried making any moves since before the wedding. Maybe because I was scared I wouldn't be good enough for her this time or maybe because the videos happened, and I didn't deserve her. I knew it, and it wouldn't take long until she knew it, too.

But I wanted her. And there was no way to deny myself when she kissed me so sweetly. Then she turned that kiss into something torrid and sensual and wild. She swiped her tongue against mine and laid her hand over my chest, caressing then scraping my skin. Feral. Fucking hot.

"Finn." And shit, the way she said my name. It was amazing.

"Lis…" I tucked her hair behind her ear. "You're beautiful."

Instead of talking, she fluttered her hand down my bare stomach, under the blanket, curled her fingers around my dick, and I almost came, but instead sucked in a breath so deep I could've floated away if I didn't want to be with her so bad.

But I had to make sure this, being together, was what she wanted. "Are you sure, Lis?"

She frowned. "Sure I want to have sex or sure I want to go bowling?"

Bowling? Now? Please, no.

"One of those I very much want to do." She grinned at me; a devilish grin that made me wonder.

"Should I get my ball?" I wanted her more than I wanted anything else in the world. Wanted her. A life with her. To bury myself inside her and never leave.

She stroked me and leaned in to lay a kiss on my collarbone.

"I think you have all the equipment we need right here." Her fist pumped faster, and I closed my eyes. "Please, Finn. Touch me. Make me yours."

There wouldn't be a need to ask twice. I probably wouldn't have survived if she did. Instead, I kissed her. Wrapped my arms around her. Nothing in the world smelled as good or tasted or felt as good as Felicity. Felicity Makenzie. My wife.

I stilled her hand because there wasn't any way I was going to last unless she stopped, and I wanted to please her, to show her how she affected me. But I had to slow things down.

"Come here." I twisted her over top of me, then onto her back next to me. Then I looked at her. Gazed down like a fool who couldn't think past how pretty she was. "Lis…"

I pressed my lips against hers, soft at first, but when she traced my mouth with her tongue, the world went hazy and desperation along with need welled inside me. She was too beautiful. Too perfect. And time was too fleeting. I could feel it.

She pulled away from the kiss and stared at me. Opened her mouth then closed it and grinned. "Can I…?"

"Anything you want." Because no way in hell would I ever be strong enough to deny her.

She sat up and pushed me onto my back. And at this rate, she wasn't going to have to touch me for something earth-shattering to occur. My world had already tilted, begun to spin out of control.

"I want you." And the way she said it, made my heart pound just a little harder. Or maybe it was her hand on my chest. Or the leg she swung over to straddle my hips. Or the line of kisses she brushed from my earlobe to my chin.

My hands landed on her hips because she shooed them away from anywhere and everywhere else I tried to touch her. The torture was exquisite. Electric. Her hips ground against my dick, and I sucked in a breath.

"You like that?" She grinned and did it again.

"Uh-huh." Because words were too much to manage with my wife. I loved thinking of her that way, on top of me, pushing her pussy into my cock, smiling like she'd invented the move. She bent to take my nipple between her teeth and twist, not gently but just hard enough that I felt it in my entire body. "Fuck, Lis."

She lifted her head, eyes twinkling. "Oh, I intend to."

And like the goddess she was, she sat up, shucked her shirt, and didn't push me away when I circled her nipple with my tongue then sucked it, holding her around the waist and shifting my hips to increase the friction between my dick and her pussy.

I'd had plenty of sex, more than my fair share probably, and any number of women had sat on me, but this…my wife…our house…there probably wasn't much chance anything in my life would ever be so perfect again. Even when she pulled away, pushed me back, and slithered down my body until she flicked her tongue out to lick my dick from base to tip. When she took me into her mouth, I gasped, held onto the blanket with white-knuckled fists, and tried not to come, but…fuck. I waited to pull her away, almost too long, then flipped us over.

Plenty of favor to return. To drive her mad with my mouth. I slipped her panties down her legs then dragged my hands up her thighs, fingertips against skin as I nudged her legs apart and stared. Nothing about this woman wasn't beautiful. And I wanted to kiss it all. Every inch of her.

I leaned forward and teased her nipples, one with my tongue, the other with my hand, then kissed and sucked my way down her belly until she writhed and tried to reach to pleasure herself.

Not on my watch she wasn't. I drew her hands away and held them, sucked one finger until she whimpered then lowered my head to her clit, swirled my tongue over her, and she half-moaned, half-gasped and tangled her hand into my hair and bent her knees, pushing her pussy up. When I slipped a finger, then another inside her, so wet, so fucking perfect, she cried out and rocked against every slide and flick.

Everything she did, made me want her more, made me want her to want me more. Her body went tense, and she tried to push me away, "Please, Finn. I want to come while you fuck me."

But then she clenched her legs and held me in place. Her body pitched and tightened, and she cried out my name, gasping, riding my fingers as I pumped them in and out of her.

Hot.

Fucking incredible.

Mine.

When she stopped writhing and moved languidly against me, I lifted my head, and she smiled. "Fuck me, now."

The three best words in the English language, especially the way Felicity said them.

I reached into the bedside table for a condom and rolled it on then smiled down at her. She ran her hand over my cheek. Stared into my eyes like there was some secret we were about to share. And heaven help me, I wanted that secret.

When I pushed inside of her, she wrapped her legs around my hips, locked her ankles, and held on. I slid deeper.

"I wish we could stay like this forever." Her voice was soft, wistful, as if she knew the end was near for us. I held on tighter.

"Me, too." I moved again, and she closed her eyes as I leaned in to kiss her. She had full pouty lips that deserved all the kisses, and my mission in life, from that moment forward, was to make sure she got them.

Instead of pounding into her, the way my body craved, I moved slow, every thrust punctuated by a kiss, a touch, a soft breath, or a look. Exquisite torture. "Is it always going to be like this?"

I closed my eyes and let her soft words roll over me before I answered. "I hope so."

"Me, too." She kissed my throat, nibbled the skin, sucked hard, then soft, then hard again, and I couldn't hold on anymore. My hips moved faster even though my brain wanted to make this last all day.

I waited until her body went stiff and she cried out, clutched my shoulders, and squeezed my hips with her legs before I let go. "Lis…" For as long as I lived, there'd never be enough time with her. Naked or otherwise. "I love you."

And I always would.

10

Felicity

Finn standing in the back of the room, in the room at all, did nothing to calm my rattled nerves. Had the opposite effect enough my hands trembled, and my vision blurred so that the room swam.

Doing a reading, especially one of my more recent books where it seemed every few pages was a love scene, wasn't for the faint of heart on a normal day and most especially when the muse for said love scenes was standing with his arms crossed and his shoulder leaned against a shelf. I stuttered through the passage.

But I made it through, finished my obligatory public appearance, signed a bunch of books, then walked out with Sofia on one side and Finn on the other. He hadn't spoken since we left the store, and I spent the whole ride sitting beside Sofia hoping that he'd lost his ability to comment on what I'd read.

'You guys okay?" Sofia side-glanced me then rear-view mirrored him.

"Fine." But I sounded like I'd just sucked in a long breath of helium.

"I'm good." And he sounded like he'd just taken a shot to the balls.

Sofia chuckled. "Okay." Thankfully, she switched subjects.

"No more appearances until after the holidays and only a couple until the official release in March. But then it's a full tour." Sofia managed my career so I was free to write whenever the urge struck without having to worry about missing appearances and social media obligations.

"A tour?"

Sofia filled him in, and I stared out the window until he laid a hand on my shoulder. Then I almost jumped out of the car because reading the scene I just read, my niche was steamy love scenes and complex storylines, and having Finn touch me had the same heart-throbbing effect on me.

"You okay?" Sofia shot me another sideways glance.

"Fine." Nothing a few minutes alone with a vibrator…or my husband, my mind wasn't playing fair, wouldn't cure.

Sofia cocked her head and twisted her lips, her I'm-not-buying-your-lies look. "Okay."

Thankfully, they chattered among themselves until we got back to my place. She didn't cut the engine, and I almost wished she would. I was too on edge, too wound up to be alone with Finn. "You want to come in?"

I pleaded with my eyes, but she ignored me.

"Can't. Got things to do. People to see." Finn thanked

her for the ride and climbed out, then she grabbed a fistful of my shirt and twisted, pulling until we were almost nose to nose. "You need to go in there and stake your claim on that guy. I recommend you do it naked, but..." She shrugged. "If you let him go, this time it's your own fault."

My mouth dropped open. "What the hell are you talking about? He's getting married."

She jerked me in again. "He's already married, you moron." She said it like moe-ron. "To you. And you two seem to be the only two people in the world who don't get that."

She shook her head and let me go. "Come on now, Flis, the whole time you were reading from your book, you stared at him, and he stared back. The two of you raised the temp in that room by a good fifty degrees. I was sweating, I can tell you that." If she had one of those old-fashioned painted fans, she would've used it for her dramatic, always dramatic, purposes.

"Did you even know there were other people in the room?" She chuckled. "Because as someone who was most definitely watching you watch him and vice versa, it really didn't seem like it to the rest of us."

"Of course, I knew you were all there." Far as I was concerned, she was losing it.

"Didn't look like it to anybody else." She'd been my best friend all these years, and I trusted her with my career, my friendship, with almost every detail of my life. But this time, she was wrong.

Right?

"Look, Flis, if you want him, you have to speak up. You have to tell him." Oh, if only life was so simple.

She let me go and waited until I'd smoothed the wrinkles she'd put into my blouse before she spoke again. Softer but more impactful, "He came back for you."

She had that wistful tone I always imagined the supporting character in every story I wrote using to get her point across.

I used the dry, you-know-nothing-main character tone. "He came back to get divorced."

I rolled my eyes at the romantic notions in her head. Maybe she spent too much time reading my novels or maybe she should've been the one writing them, because real life never worked out this way. Even if I wished I could write the ending for this one.

He left me for a reason. And he'd only come back now to make the leaving permanent. Not a fact I could forget as well as Sofia could ignore.

"He could've handled all this with a phone call, but he's here. And you're going to regret it for the rest of your life if you don't go in there and tell him how you feel." She smiled softly as I was about to deny, deny, deny. "I want you to be happy, Felicity, and he made you happy. At least think about it."

So, I did. It was all I thought about. All afternoon. And I couldn't really help it that when I imagined talking to him about my feelings, I pictured us in bed, sweaty and breathing hard, limbs tangled, bodies still joined.

And those thoughts did nothing to calm my need. Neither did standing in the kitchen space with him, bumping into each other and not speaking as I made a salad and he cooked a pizza until I turned from the sink and stopped to watch as he bent to check the pizza through the little glass window in the oven door.

"Tell me you love her, Finn." Maybe if I heard the words from his mouth, I could wrap my head around not only the idea but the act of behaving myself.

He straightened and took a breath before he turned to face me. "Why?"

He didn't say it. He didn't tell me he loved her. He didn't move away from me when I stepped closer. "Because I…need to hear you say it."

I laid my hand on his chest. "Because you're married to me, and the line between right and wrong is getting really blurry."

I ended on a whisper because his eyes went dark, smoldered, and I couldn't breathe.

There was something to be said for small kitchens and soon-to-be ex-husbands who weren't yet ex-husbands. The way he lifted his hand to cup my cheek and lowered his head made the world narrow down to the strip of space between us. "Lis."

I thought he was going to kiss me, closed my eyes in preparation, but opened them when his forehead pressed against mine.

"Shit." I wanted to cry. He hadn't said the words. But he didn't kiss me either. I pulled away. Humiliated. Exhausted. Dying inside.

And because the heroine never stuck around, and I was huge on dramatic exits, I ran to my room. I shut myself in.

I planned to die of starvation in there since I hadn't waited long enough for the pizza to get done.

I threw myself backward on my bed. Why on Earth did I listen to Sofia? Not a question I hadn't spoken before, but one I should've learned from a long time ago. More than once, more than a hundred times, listening to her had ended up with me doubting everything about myself. Even if later, it turned into something positive, and it had a lot, but it couldn't this time. Not this time.

He knocked on the door, and I wished I could disappear. It would be easier than seeing him. It would be less painful than looking into the face of my humiliation. And maybe if I stayed quiet enough, he would think I died and would just go away.

Instead, he opened the door and walked in like he owned the place. Like if I ever lifted the arm from my face to look at him, I wouldn't kick him out.

The mattress sank next to me, and his breath warmed my cheek while his fingertip ran the length of my arm between my elbow and palm where it laid over my eyes before he circled my wrist and pulled it away.

And because I couldn't bear to look at him, not because I was immature, I squeezed my eyes shut and turned my head away. But even I wasn't strong enough to resist when he curled his finger under my chin and guided my chin toward him. "Please, Lis."

He let his finger drag down my throat, and had I not already humiliated myself, I would've sighed. My heart racing was all the indication I would give that I wanted him.

"Lis…" His voice was soft, pleading, and I opened my eyes to the storm clouds in his. "I don't…,"

"Don't love her? Don't want me?" Well aware I sounded needy and unable to do a damned thing about it, I waited for his answer.

"Don't love her. Don't want to hurt you." He paused and I looked away until he added, "I don't want to leave you. Don't want to walk out of this bedroom until I've kissed every inch of your body, until I've worshiped you the way you deserve, until I'm the only man you ever think of for the rest of your life."

Boy, did I have news for him? And instead of just saying okay and stripping down to naked, I took a slow breath. "What's stopping you?"

Now he looked away, stared at the ceiling then closed his eyes. "Beth Cooper. I'm marrying Beth Cooper."

What.

The.

Fuck.

All the hormones begging me to forget his pending nuptials slammed shut and died. And then the mean part of me, the one who didn't care about Beth Cooper's feelings or that I would be the other woman and she would be able to claim I'd hurt her, the part of me that heard her name in the same way a normal person heard Ted Bundy or Jeffrey Dahmer, said she deserved whatever I did to her. Because she'd used her new fame and her press pass and her editing software to make me the first poster girl of the Glouster scandal. My video, with a thin black bouncing box over my eyes and two blurry spots where my equally bouncing boobs should've been, was the first played on national news channels. Because of Beth Cooper.

I chuckled. Then laughed. Then guffawed. Finn stared until I calmed. "Of course, you're marrying Beth Cooper. Of course, because of the almost four billion women in the world, only Beth Fucking Cooper makes sense."

Then I turned toward him, threw my leg over the top of his cock, gave it a rub, and lowered myself to a level it would take years and an Eiffel Tower size ladder to climb out of. "But if you think that makes me want to fuck you less right now, you're wrong."

"Fucking hell, Lis." The husky tone in his voice, the way he pulled his lip between his teeth, oh, the heat of his gaze scorched my skin. And I wanted more. I wasn't going to be able to stop soon. Fortunately, Finn could. Always. Either this guy had the willpower of a nun or he just didn't find me attractive enough to want me the way he used to.

He laid his hand on my calf, stilling any motion I might've made, then rolled onto his side so we were almost chest to chest and my knee rested on his hip. One pelvic tilt and a lot of courage would tell me one way or the other if I still...had it, but the prospect of the humiliation of another rejection kept me mostly still.

My mind whirled. Would a pre-divorce bang be so out of line? Would a long, slow, goodbye screw be considered wrong on any level?

He closed his eyes. "Since I met you, Lis, all I've wanted to be is good enough to be with you. I didn't have money. Or a good name. In a relationship, I bring one thing to the table."

Oh yeah. And it was quite the thing. I smiled. Remembering the talent with which he used the thing he brought to the table. Vividly. My leg twitched against it. But it wasn't all he had to offer. I wanted to tell him, but he continued.

"And even when I went off course, you never made me feel like I wasn't enough. You made me feel like I was everything." Because he was. Then. Now. Probably always would be.

"But I can't be with you, Lis, because if I do, I'll be happy…" he brushed his hand down my cheek. "So happy, but I won't be the man you deserve because that guy wouldn't use you to break his commitment to Beth."

And that just burned my ass. "What about your commitment to me? You didn't have a problem breaking that."

I yanked my leg away and sat up.

"I'm not that guy anymore. And I would die to take it back, to not hurt you or make you feel like…" He shook his head, breath heavy and eyes dark. And my blood went cold then burned through my veins.

"Well, isn't that just freaking dandy? Ten years later, you get your shit together for *Beth Cooper*." If I had anything handy, I might've thrown it at him. Instead, I walked out of the bedroom, slipped my shoes on, and grabbed my coat.

"Where are you going?"

"I need to get some air." And a life apparently. Because dammit, he'd gone out and found one that didn't include me. It was time I did the same.

One Decade Ago

WATER SLOSHED over the side of the tub, and I giggled as Finn's fingertip circled my nipple. The water was still mostly warm, but I was on fire. Again.

"You're getting me all wet." He was on his knees outside the tub, shirt and lap soaked.

"Back at ya." He grinned, and I could've swooned. "You could just get undressed and get in here with me."

My bath had started before he came home, when all of my muscles were achy and strained from the three days of non-stop sex before he had to leave this morning for a meeting with the football coaches and staff.

"The water's cold now." And even though he smiled, it didn't reach his eyes. Didn't transform his face. He stood and bent to kiss me before he walked from the bathroom to the bedroom.

I stood, stepped out of the water and slipped on the tile floor, smacking my head against the side of the tub. "Fuck!"

He ran back in to find me bent at an odd angle with blood pouring from a cut on my scalp. He snatched the towel I'd planned to use to dry off and held it against my head.

"Are you okay?" He helped me sit up then pulled the towel away for a look. "Are you hurt anywhere else?"

He took my hand and put it on the towel.

"Hold this." Then, he ran his palms over everywhere else. "Anything hurt?"

"I'm naked on the bathroom floor, my head's bleeding, and my husband is only interested in my ouchies. My pride is hurt." I shoved his hands away. "The rest of me is fine."

Except for the cool wooziness making my bathroom spin so that I swayed into him.

He took control of the towel at my head and peeked under it as he held me, naked and dripping against him.

"You need a couple stitches." Because of course I did.

"And to get checked out because you might have a concussion." He held up his hand. "How many fingers?"

"Eight and two thumbs."

He shook his head. "Smartass."

With my luck, now that I was happier than I'd ever been, I'd probably just given myself a brain aneurysm and had seconds left to live. But before the angel of death had the opportunity to come knocking, Finn helped me get dressed, held my hand when the doctor sutured my head closed, waited in the hall during my CT scan, then drove me home after the hospital doctor gave the all-clear.

When we walked inside our house, he led me to the bedroom, then unfastened my coat and slipped it down my arms, unraveled my scarf and tossed it on the chair, and pulled off my gloves to fling them so they landed with the scarf. All the while side-stepping my grabby hands. "Come on. The doctor said to rest."

"Finn..." I growled his name and reached for him again. "Fine."

Not fine at all, but salvageable at least. "Will you rest with me, at least?"

He nodded and once we were settled with my head on his chest and his arms around me, I pressed a kiss against his throat. If I looked up, I might have seen the sadness in his eyes, maybe even tears, but I didn't and fell asleep instead. By the time I woke, the sun had set, and my room was dark. Finn's side of the bed was cold.

I stood, wishing for an aspirin, then walked out into the living room. From our house, we could see the school's back side. The peak of the steepled ministry building. The dome over the basketball gymnasium. And he stood at the window staring, shoulders shaking. I touched his back, and he sucked in a shallow breath.

"You okay?"

"Coach said I'm getting kicked out of school." He didn't turn to look at me, but his voice was thick, soft, broken. "I'm never going to be a doctor."

His shoulders curled in. "I'm everything all those people said about me, all those foster families that said I would never be anything. They were right."

Oh, fuck. My heart broke for him.

"I'll talk to my dad." I wrapped myself around him, scooted until I could see his face. "Finn."

He looked down, and his tears shattered me. "Just leave me alone, Lis. Please. I don't want to talk about this with you."

"Okay." Not okay, I wanted to help him, hold him, tell him it didn't matter at least, but in the absence of permission, maybe I really could talk to Dad. I unwrapped my arms, bundled up for the cold, and walked straight to the street lined with expensive houses that all had maids. When I got to the big one at the end, I stomped up the porch steps and banged on the door. I could hear his TV inside. He was probably reading a newspaper or something in the back of the house so I banged again, and after a few minutes, he opened the door so I could breeze past him.

I was four steps inside when he shut the door and turned to me. "Felicity. You okay?"

I scoffed. "Funny you should ask. Because I'm a hundred percent *not* okay. You kicked Finn out of school?"

He shook his head.

"It wasn't just me, sweetheart. The board voted. All the boys involved were expelled." Funny, but a man who valued integrity and honor couldn't look me in the eyes. "He can appeal."

"Did you fight for him at all? Did you stand up and tell them he didn't know?" I'd had that talk/argument with him already.

Dad glared at me and wrinkled his forehead as if he couldn't believe I was asking. "I'm not going to fight for the man who took your reputation and flushed it down the drain."

"Oh, Dad." The disappointment was thick in my stomach and churning away.

"His own fraternity brothers said he knew the cameras were there for months." And Dad matched my feeling with his own tone. "And he took you there anyway, Flis. He knew. Beth Cooper, Susie Ranes, Alicia Bates. They all asked for him to be kicked out."

"Beth Cooper?" The same woman who was all over TV, chasing down interviews with victims, had gone to the chancellors against Finn?

"She deserves the same justice you do." I wanted to hit

something, to shake my dad and make him understand how important this was to me. "The final vote's next week."

He took my hands in his.

"Please, honey, leave him now. Don't wait for the fallout of this. That fucking video has been on TV all week." He lowered his head. "I had to watch my little girl getting… screwed by this guy on fucking CNN. So no, Felicity, I did not defend him. He's lucky I don't go over there and beat his ass."

My dad never said the F-word. In all my 21 years of life, I'd never heard it pass his lips until now. And he'd never had a violent moment. Of course, neither had I ever disappointed him in such a big way. Shit.

I was an English major. Not prelaw. I didn't have an argument in me since I couldn't deny anything he said. "He's my husband, Dad."

It was all I had as a defense.

"Yeah. I know." But Dad was one of the great thinkers of my time, one of the men who asked questions designed to make a person think. It was his skill. "Your loyalty is admirable, and I hope he's done some other thing to show you he deserves it, but at some point, you're going to have to ask yourself if it was all worth it. And I hope it is. I hope he's true and honest and honorable, and he treats you the way you deserve with all the love in the world. But if it turns out the answer isn't yes and all this wasn't worth it, come find me. We'll pick up the pieces. But I can't watch you be with him."

He shrugged one shoulder and a tear slipped down his cheek.

"What does that mean? *You're* dumping me?" Dads didn't get to dump their daughters. But mine lifted his head, sniffed once and adjusted his glasses, then did it.

"I'll be here when you need me." He walked to the door and held it open. My invitation to exit. "Right now, you don't."

I walked out. What the hell just happened? I'd gone there to defend my husband with the Chancellor of students and ended up being shown out by my dad. "Fuck."

Well, wasn't this just quite the day?

11

Finn

$\mathcal{I}$ waited an hour before I started to freak out. Another 20 minutes before it occurred to me that she'd left without her purse or her phone or her keys. Ten more before it occurred to me that I could use her phone to call Sofia.

She answered and music blared in the background. "Hey, Flissy's phone. Which must mean this is the future Mr. Beth Cooper." She laughed at her own joke. "Because Flissy is with me, and we are getting our drink on because, whoo, she is pissed at you."

"I'm not pissed at anyone and it's Mr. Dr. Beth Cooper or Dr. Mr. Beth Cooper. Ask him which one it is. I tried to figure it out when I looked him up online, but couldn't figure it all out," Felicity's words slurred in the background. And then her voice was in my ear. "Hey, you can go to bed because I'm not coming home tonight. I'm going to find someone who doesn't require batteries or permission to rock my world. And by rock my world, I mean screw me cross-eyed and immobile. I want to see heaven by morning."

"Oh, yeah?" No. I couldn't go find her and offer my services in that respect. It would be wrong.

"You bet your ass I am." She scoffed into the phone. "Because you want Beth Cooper. Fine. But I'm not going to sit around and wait for you anymore. I'm sorry. But I need action in my business…areas."

Oh shit. "Okay."

But if she asked me, no way would I be able to turn her down.

"Finn?" Her voice was soft, a breath, the most erotic sound I've ever heard.

"Yeah?"

"Is it okay if I think about you while…"

Fuck! "Where are you at?"

I'd drive across the country for this.

"I'm not telling you so you can come here, and cock block me." Her voice broke. "I need this, Finn. I need someone to touch me and to want me. Please just let me have it."

I wasn't sure what she was asking me, but the answer was yes. Hell yes. This time when I asked, I didn't leave room for argument. "Tell me where you are, Lis."

She gave me the name of the bar and was still sitting at the counter when I walked in and stood behind her to lean in and whisper in her ear. "You're beautiful, and I want you."

To hell with being the guy who deserved her, to being the guy who couldn't sleep with the wife I loved because I owed the fiancée blackmailing me into marriage some weird loyalty.

She turned her stool to face me. "Kiss me."

It wasn't a dare or a challenge. It was Felicity asking for what she wanted. For what I told her I would give her.

I took her face in my hands, stroked her cheeks with my thumbs until her eyelids fluttered, memorized her face again then lowered my head. I wanted soft and sweet, a prelude to how I planned to love her as soon as I got her home, but she curled her fingers into my shirt and pulled me in then held me there.

When she pulled back, she chewed her lower lip. "I don't want to have sex."

Parts of me were going to be unforgivably blue since I'd done nothing but think about sex with her since I called her on Sofia's phone. "Okay."

"I mean, I do. Just not tonight because I want to remember it and I want to be good, and I'm too drunk for either of those things." I almost offered to remember it enough for both of us, but she chuckled. "I guess we could capture it all on video."

She threw her head back and laughed while I watched. After a minute, a full, loud minute, she sobered and fought for control with twitching lips and an inability to meet my gaze. "Too soon? It's been ten years."

"Lis…" If only she knew. And tomorrow, before we did anything else, I would tell her the price we'd pay together if

I broke my engagement with Beth, and I couldn't sleep with Felicity if I didn't.

"Take her home, Finn." Sofia's voice came from behind me. "She's taking up valuable real estate next to me."

She kissed Felicity's cheek. "How is super-hot bar guy," she winked at Dakota who was standing behind the bar, "supposed to slip into the stool if you're still sitting on it? Go home."

Felicity nodded and staggered to her feet. "Thanks, Sofe. For everything."

"Have fun." Sofia nodded and winked as Felicity staggered out of the bar in front of me.

I led her to the car and helped her into the passenger seat. As I slid in behind the wheel, she leaned her head back and stared at me. "Finn, I have to tell you something."

I nodded unsure my morals would stand up to a soul-bearing confession from her, but sure I wanted to hear what she had to say. If she loved me, or if she didn't, I needed to know so I could decide what to do with the information, cherish it or not. Because loving her back had never been my choice. "I have to pee."

I laughed. "Well, let's get you home."

When I pulled up, she ran into the house and was waiting for me by the time I convinced myself to go inside. I considered not going in. No matter what she said, there was no way I would be a good enough man to walk away from her and let her get on with her life.

She stood just inside the bedroom door and crooked her finger. "Come here."

"Are you sure?" But I was already on my way.

"You're married to me. That makes you mine. Unless you're mad I burned the divorce papers, then…" I stopped walking. Was she looking for an excuse for us not to be together tonight? "Yes or no. Are you pissed that we never got divorced, and it means you're more mine than hers?"

I took too long to answer, and she pushed the door shut. I leaned my head against it. "I wish I would've known sooner."

I don't know if she heard my whisper or if she changed her mind about letting me decide, but she flung the door open, grabbed me by the shirt, and pushed me against the wall. Her hands slipped to my chest and around to clasp behind my neck as I circled her waist and kissed her like I'd been waiting my whole life to do it.

Her lips parted, and I slipped my tongue inside. It was explosive, enchanting and she was so fucking delicious. She was everything I ever wanted. But I couldn't sleep with her. I had to end things with Beth first. And before I could do that, I had to tell Felicity the ramifications of denying Beth this wedding. And Felicity needed to be sober enough to understand first. That wasn't going to happen tonight. Nothing was going to happen tonight.

I pulled back and held her against me. Let my heart and my breath slow before I tried to speak. "Let me hold you tonight, okay?"

She looked up and smiled, and I almost didn't finish speaking. "Just lay beside me, and let me… We can dream about each other."

She nodded. "Okay."

And we spent the night cuddled together, not talking,

not kissing, just being together. And it was almost as perfect as sex.

By the time I woke in the morning, she was already awake and staring at me. "Hi."

I pushed my hair back so I could see all of her face and smiled. "Hi."

"I'm not drunk anymore." I nodded because I didn't know where she was going with it.

"I'm hungover. And tired. But not drunk." Her eyelashes fluttered against her cheeks. "Thank you for not taking advantage of me last night."

Oh. I wasn't expecting that.

"It's okay. Holding you was enough for last night." Great, now I sounded like I expected more. And while I wanted more, so much more, I didn't want her to think I expected it. "I mean…I like holding you and sleeping beside you. Listening to you breathe."

She closed her eyes and blew out a breath as she ran her finger over my lips. "Shh."

Another breath. And I knew this was going to suck. "You're getting married, Finn. And I can't…you're marrying someone else. And that's okay. I get it. It's hard being alone. But you can't stay here anymore."

She swallowed hard. "I'm not…strong enough to…you have to go."

"Because you want me?" I wasn't taunting her. Hearing her say the words would give me the strength to tell her the truth or set her free depending on which way this went.

Her sigh was long and deep. "Because my claim to you is expired. Because Beth Cooper wants to marry you."

Her voice cracked. "Because I have a memory of our time together before that is so...perfect and so...exquisite...this is never going to be that. It'll never live up to it. It'll just end up ruining both then and now."

This was a hold my beer kind of moment. A challenge extended. "What if it's better?"

She swallowed hard. "Then it would kill me to let you go again."

A tear slipped over her nose and landed on my arm where she'd laid her head. "I don't know if I can make it through a second time, Finn."

If I would've known last night that this would be how we started today, I wouldn't have gone to sleep. I would've stayed awake, watched her sleep, refreshed my mind with all the little details about her, held her tighter, kissed her longer.

I nodded. "Okay."

There was nothing I could deny her. Nothing I would ever even consider denying her. Her happiness was all I cared about, and if this was what she wanted, then...okay. But first, she needed to know...how I felt. I tightened my arms around her. "Lis, before I go...I never got over you. And everything I've done since I left was to prove that leaving was the right thing for both of us, so I could come back one day, and you'd be proud of who I am."

"Even marrying Beth?"

I smiled. Leave it to Felicity to catch that. "No. That's about something else. I mean with the rest of my life. I worked hard in med school. I made sure I was at the top of my class. I kept my head down. Did the work so if I ever ran into you, I could introduce myself as *Dr.* Makenzie and you'd be impressed."

She nodded. "I am impressed, Dr. Makenzie."

But it wasn't enough. I had to leave her again. And I didn't want to now any more than I did back then. "Do you know my favorite night when we were married before?"

What was I doing? This trip down memory lane was going to kill me.

"Naked Tuesday? Wet and wild Wednesday?" She chuckled like we weren't breaking up. Again.

I swallowed a couple times to get rid of the lump in my throat so I could speak. "The night we put all the blankets and pillows on the floor in front of the TV and laughed, told jokes, made out."

She twisted her lips. "We didn't even have sex that night."

"It wasn't always about sex for me." True, no matter what she thought or how my previous behavior made it look. "That night, I was really happy. I thought if we could just have that every once in a while, it would be enough to get us through anything. It felt normal and I didn't get a lot of that before. So, it was… one of the top eleven best nights of my life."

"Finn." She whispered my name or maybe I imagined her saying it, but I savored the sound. "We didn't have sex that night because Ryder just beat your ass. We were married for 11 days. You got kicked out of school that day for good and I didn't…"

She turned away. "I didn't know if I could be with someone who was kicked out of school."

The air whooshed out of me like she'd hit me. She didn't hold me and laugh with me because she loved me. She was holding back because she didn't love me enough. Nothing I thought about us back then was right. Not from her side anyway. And the second great heartbreak of my life was directly connected to the first.

One Decade Ago

IN TWO MINUTES, I was officially going to be late. And of all the things I couldn't afford to be, late for this meeting with the board of chancellors wasn't it. I was going to save my own ass, to rat out my best friend and put an end to the first fraternity established at Glouster. I was going to take a deal that would keep me in school or at least let me get into another school.

Lis made the deal. She went to her dad and pleaded, begged, and cried. Now I had exactly one chance to tell all.

I should've taken the car, but I wanted to walk so I could clear my head, organize my thoughts, figure out what to say to do the best I could to save myself.

I passed teachers, students, people who had no idea what I was about to do, although unless they'd slept through the entirety of the last two weeks, there was no way anyone I passed didn't know what I'd *done*.

The voice. The "Hey, buddy, where you headed," made my guts ache.

I didn't have to guess what Ryder was doing on campus right now, he'd been kicked out two weeks ago without being allowed an explanation. I also didn't need to wonder if catching me at this exact moment was a coincidence. Ryder didn't do coincidence.

"I have a meeting." But he knew that.

"Don't do this, man."

That he could ask after what he did, that he used all of us to make money, that he humiliated not only us but all those women, was a sign Ryder wasn't the kind of guy who was going to learn.

I didn't answer because I didn't know what to say. How could he ask me not to save myself and the others?

"Finn…" He stopped walking, I turned, and he punched. I didn't see it coming. I wouldn't have expected it. I wouldn't have expected that he would have jumped on top of me and pounded his fist into my face over and over again. Or that he would've stood over me, spat, and bent down to haul me up by my shirt. "We were friends, and I would never sell you out."

The fact that he actually had 'sold me out' when he sold those videos of me seemed to have escaped him.

He let go and my head banged hard against the concrete sidewalk. He walked off and I watched as the light slowly faded away.

I woke later, after the sun set, in an alley. My thoughts were broken into as small increments as I could whittle them down.

I missed the meeting.

Felicity would never forgive me.

The school would never forgive me.

And for the two or three minutes I remained conscious, I couldn't forgive myself. I deserved this, I just wished he would've waited a few hours.

The next time I opened my eye, only one worked, I was in a hospital room. Alone. I was hooked to a machine. "Am I okay?"

My words sounded like 'grr grr grkay?' but it didn't matter because no one heard me anyway.

I tried to sit up, tried to move, but I managed only to wiggle a finger as I tried to reposition myself. What the hell. My body wouldn't respond to a single one of my commands.

But then it came back to me. Ryder. The meeting. Fuck.

And I needed to get home. To explain to Felicity why I'd missed the chance to throw myself at the mercy of Glouster University and their council of leaders led by her father.

This time, I pulled myself up. And a nurse rushed into the room. "Hey! Hey!"

She pushed my shoulder until I finally relaxed against the pillow behind me. But she also underestimated the urgency of my being able to leave. As soon as she let go, I moved again. This time she shoved me without any regard for my pain. "Listen. We found your ID. We're trying to get a hold of someone."

It hurt to breathe, and the talking was probably going to be my final act of courage, but I had to try.

"My wife." My mouth felt broken. "Her number's in my phone."

She handed me my cell from the table by my wallet. My broken cell. Fuck! I wasn't going to win any good husband awards because I didn't know my wife's number.

No. This couldn't be happening. We'd only been married nine days. Nine glorious days with Felicity. Who would probably end up thinking I left her because no way her dad didn't call to tell her I didn't show up.

I needed to go home. Needed to see Felicity.

The hospital was probably one of the hardest places I'd ever tried to sneak out of. Someone in scrubs was always walking down the hallway, and I couldn't take the elevator for the obvious reasons, well, I didn't have my own clothes, and my ass was hanging out of the back of my little gown. But I made it out and made it home to find Felicity on the sofa, crying.

She hadn't even looked up when I walked in. I sat beside her, with no idea what I looked like or how she would react when she looked up, but I certainly expected her anger. "You missed the meeting."

Her eyes, normally sparkling and happy, burned with anger and disbelief.

"Lis." Did she not see the bruises? The stitches beside my eye? My busted lip?

"They kicked you out, Finn." She nodded then scoffed then buried her head in her hands. "Kicked you out."

"What about Jameson and Keaton? What about Ryder?" They'd all been offered the same deal.

"I don't give a fuck about them." Her mouth compressed into a thin line. Her eyes narrowed. It was like her face was shutting me out, one expression at a time. "I cared about you."

Cared. Past tense.

I looked at the room. The blankets on the floor. The candles burned down. The DVD cases on the table. Then I looked at Felicity. Sheer black robe. Heels she'd kicked off on the floor beside the sofa. Eyes red from crying.

"Lis." I had to explain. "I tried to be there."

She sighed. "Do you think I did this to myself?"

She wouldn't even look at me. "Lis, please. Ryder…"

"Went in and took your deal. He admitted everything, but he…" She pursed her lips and stood to pace in front of me. Kicking the blankets and pillows to the corner of the room as she made her first pass. "He took you down with him. Saved Keaton, gave Jameson an out, but he made sure that when he threw you under it, the bus didn't just run over you, it dragged you a couple thousand feet."

I would've sold my soul to have started the day over again. To not have her look at me like I'd disappointed her. For just one more minute of happiness with her.

"What did your dad say?" He was the guy who'd promised to help me. The one whose eyes I would have to look into for as long as his daughter loved me.

"Before or after Beth Cooper came busting into the meeting, and they let her play the entirety of one video, then read out the names of all the other girls?" She paced a couple more laps from one side of the room to the other before she continued. I would have spoken, but my guts were twisted, my head aching, and I wanted to die.

"You want to know which video she played? Or how many times you looked right at the camera? I never noticed but she counted." She stared hard, and my shoulders sagged under the weight of it. "Do you want to know?"

"I never lied about knowing the cameras were there." Weak. Lame. Not much of a defense. But it was all I had.

She nodded. "I guess you didn't."

She sat beside me. "And I didn't really care about it until I got out of class early and decided to go to the hearing to support you. I thought what I was asking you to do would be easier if you saw me there."

She shook her head but took my hand in hers. "I knew how hard it would be to blame Ryder. I saw you guys for the last four years. Best friends. And Keaton and Jameson… I knew it would be hard and I just wanted to be there for you."

Her voice wavered and tears pooled in her eyes. "Instead," she sucked in a long breath and ran her hand through her hair, "I had to watch my husband fuck *her*."

Beth showed her own video. This was a woman who knew shock value and how to use it.

"Shit." I looked down because meeting her eyes was too much to bear. "I didn't know he would…"

"Bullshit. You said yourself you knew the cameras were there. And if you didn't know he would put them online, you at least knew he could." She pulled her hand away from mine and folded it with the other in her lap. "God, Finn. You want to know the worst part?"

I did not. "Yeah."

"The worst part is, I had this great night planned for us.

I set everything up this morning I was so excited. And…
part of me still wants to fix the pillows and turn on the TV,
lay beside you. I thought even though we would be celebrating for you, you might be sad over your friends."

She looked at me then closed her eyes as if it was too
much to look at me. Too hard. "And I'm so pathetic, I want
you to comfort me now."

And I pulled her against me. We could work through
this. I had that kind of faith in us. What I didn't have was
much time left to prove it. I pulled her against me and
smoothed her hair.

"For tonight, can we just…?" She nodded to the blanket
and pillows. "We can deal with every other thing
tomorrow."

"Yeah." I wanted to change out of my hospital gown
first, but I didn't want to leave her.

I didn't know how much time I had left with her, but if
this was going to be my last night, I wanted to remember
every second. Every smile. Every flutter of her lashes.
Every kiss I could sneak in.

12

Felicity

he admission that I might not have loved him as much as he thought I did back then was almost as hard as seeing his suitcase by my front door. As knowing the roads were icy. Or that the night was cold. Or that he was leaving again and this time because I told him to go.

So, as he stood slipping his arms into his coat then twisting his scarf around his neck, I watched. Too scared to speak, to ask for what I wanted. Stunted by his rejection. But this was my last chance. And if I let him slip away…

"Finn." He turned, and I waited one more second. Too long. Then marched to where he stood, shoved him against the wall, and kissed him like it was the last time I would ever get to. I tangled my fingers in his hair and held him until he kissed me back and wound his arms around me, opened his mouth, turned us so I was the one pinned between him and the wall. When he pulled back and leaned his forehead against mine, I closed my eyes and caressed his scalp with my fingertips. "Stay this time. Tell her you can't marry her because you want to be with me."

What? "Please."

Seriously. What was I doing?

"Lis…" He closed his eyes and shook his head. "I have to go."

He turned to the door, picked up his suitcase, and walked out.

My heart ached. How had I done this with this guy? Again.

I dragged myself away from the wall and was almost to the kitchen where I planned to eat all the ice cream and junk food in the house, then maybe work on the hidden bottle of vodka I kept at the very back of the freezer. I had no intention of chasing him. This was my idea. He had to go. It was the right thing. And I was about one second from telling myself to go to hell and running after him when the door opened and he stalked into the empty bedroom, came out the bathroom door, then finally turned to see me in the kitchen.

Without a word, he pulled me against him, held my face in one hand, my waist in the other, and kissed me.

"I can't marry her." He pulled back and grinned. "Because I'm married to you."

"Yeah. We're very married." And I kissed him.

"And I don't want to be blackmailed into giving you up."

We were deep into another kiss before it registered. "What? She's blackmailing you?"

He kissed a line along my jaw then his warm breath brushed my throat as he lifted his head enough to whisper, "It's always been you, Lis."

And like the magic words they were, my clothes just started falling off. My shirt landed on the back of the sofa as we walked, lips still fused together as we passed it toward the bedroom. My shoes ended up one by the bathroom door, one by the wall inside my room. My jeans beside the bed. His clothes also disappeared though I couldn't say where. But not a stitch of fabric remained between us when he laid me on the bed and leaned over to kiss me.

Time had no effect on him. His body was still etched with muscle. His hands still knew every spot to touch. And his mouth made me thankful for teeth and tongues and things I'd always taken for granted.

He moved onto the bed beside me and smiled. "You're still so beautiful." He ran his finger from my collarbone, between my breasts to my belly button, made a circle then retraced the path. Soft. Dizzying. And I closed my eyes to delight in the touch.

He kissed me and repeated the process while his tongue worked magic in my mouth, this time, he dipped his hand lower, skipping the part I wanted touched to run his palm over my thigh, to my knee, and back again.

"I love your skin, Lis." Then he kissed me again while he stroked the inside of my thigh and finally ran his finger over my clit. I gasped. And he didn't wait. He pushed his fingers inside me, touching, teasing, using his thumb to make small circles that built pressure low in my belly.

Heat spread through my limbs, and he swallowed my every moan and whimper, his hand making delicious circles while his kiss went from passionate to carnal, from wild to feral. He tore away to take my nipple in his mouth and my back arched. His tongue teased in concert with his fingers as his mouth pulled and my clit responded.

"I can't wait, Lis." He climbed on top of me and I wrapped my legs around him. Pulled him in. Held him there until my ignored and unused body adjusted. He was hard and hot and kissing me like we only had today. Maybe we did. Maybe tomorrow there wouldn't be an us. But I didn't care. Tomorrow could handle itself. Right now, I had the only man I'd ever wanted, the only one I would ever love.

He curled his fingers into my hair, and I moaned at the exquisite pressure. I wanted more. I wanted fire and passion and to drive him as crazy as he was making me. I tried to turn us, but he grinned. "Not this time. Next time, okay?"

If I said no, he would shift us, but we had all night. In case there was only to be this one, I was going to have plenty to remember when I needed it.

His hips thrust and I lifted mine to meet him. Primal. Needy. Desperate for more of him.

The pressure imploded. Splintered and fractured.

Above me, his body went tense and he groaned with effort before he shuddered and collapsed.

"Fuck, Lis."

I knew the feeling. I just couldn't speak it.

Finn rolled off me. "I forgot a condom, Lis."

I took health class in seventh grade. I knew that pregnancy could happen the first time. The second time. The two-hundred and ninety-fourth time. But right now, I couldn't bring myself to care.

"That's okay."

He kissed my shoulder and turned to face me. "Should we talk about this?"

Talk about the fact we'd crossed a line we couldn't uncross? Talk about what was going to happen tomorrow? Talk about Beth Cooper blackmailing him?

"No. We should rest up for round two." I pulled the side of the blanket over us and laid my head on his chest.

"Lis…"

"Shh. Don't ruin it." Tomorrow was soon enough.

And by morning, we'd discovered any and every detail we might have forgotten about each other. Rekindled the desire. Amped up the passion. Touched and tasted each other. Slept wrapped together in a tangle of limbs and blankets. But it was tomorrow. Time to face whatever was going on. And I couldn't face it naked, lying beside him.

Unfortunately, whoever picked that exact moment to knock on the door didn't care about my clothing situation. I rolled out of bed and slipped my arms into my robe. He'd already managed to slide both legs into his jeans and button the five buttons at his fly. I had a distinct and fond memory of popping those buttons open. I smiled and shot him a wink. "Be right back."

He stopped me for a kiss then grinned down as the persistent person at the door knocked again.

"I'll start the shower while you get rid of whoever that is. Then you can join me, and I'll wash your back." He wiggled his eyebrows.

But all I could think of was the 120 things we needed to say to each other so his leaving wouldn't kill me this time. "We have to talk."

"I know. We will after I wash your back, you dirty girl." He kissed me softly as the rabid knocker gave a repeat performance. "Go. I'll be waiting in the shower."

I laughed and took another kiss before I turned and walked out, shutting the door behind me. I didn't often get visitors, especially at 9 a.m. so it was either my dad or the mailman, and neither needed to get a glimpse of my bedroom. As I passed the sofa, I stuffed my shirt under a cushion then answered the door.

Beth Fucking Cooper. In the flesh. On my porch. Probably came to claim her fiancé. The man in my shower belting out the chorus to *Walk This Way.*

She walked past me. "How did you ever stand that off-key howling he does in the shower without going in and strangling him?"

She said it as if the sound of Finn's bellowing annoyed her. As if she had first-hand annoyance issues.

I ignored the tingle in my belly. So, what if she knew he sang in the shower? And there was a 50-50 chance it would be off-key. Didn't mean anything that she'd guessed it right. I shut the door behind her and crossed my arms. "What do you want?"

She rolled her eyes. "Look, I don't know what he's told you, but I'm marrying Finn tomorrow." A frown punctuated her up and down gaze. "Can I assume you have him out of your system now?"

I had no idea what to say, but I wanted to resist the guilt and shame inside me. Unfortunately, I was weak, and the guilt and shame were strong. But so was my dislike for Beth Cooper. "He's married to me. You're blackmailing him."

She laughed and spun away then spun back.

"Is that what he told you?" She scoffed. "Blackmail. Do you have any idea who I am? I'm Elizabeth Cooper, I have my own talk show that airs around the country Monday to Friday. I don't have to blackmail anyone."

Her eyes narrowed.

"He's my husband." Oh no. Weak. Any idiot could see the holes big enough to drive the Titanic through.

"Oh, please. Husband shmusband. We both know Finn isn't the kind of guy who can keep it in his pants when he's faced with," she cocked an eyebrow, "that kind of temptation, and he was your husband ten years ago. Before you threw him away." When I opened my mouth to argue, she rolled her eyes.

"Save your breath. I know. You didn't tell him to leave, but what other choice did you give him but to take your daddy's money?" She shrugged. "And thank fuck, because if he would've stayed with you, he would've never become a doctor. You would've held him back. The only good thing you did was get your dad to buy him off."

And I couldn't deny any of it. Not because it was true,

which it was, but because I was stuck on something else she said. "My daddy's money?"

Buy him off? My stomach clenched. "What the fuck are you talking about?"

She rolled her eyes. "Oh, it's been so long since I've seen such a good innocent act. Please go on and tell me how you didn't know about your dad getting Finn into USC, then Stanford, and paying for the whole thing?"

I sighed to cover my hurt, trying maybe to blow it out like spent breath. "What do you want, Beth?"

She wanted her fiancé. And I didn't have to be Einstein to know it.

She laughed. "What do I want?"

It took a minute, enough time for her to run her finger along the bookshelf, to stare at a picture of me and Dad at the beach on a winter day with my hair blowing where it stuck out from under a pom-topped hat and Dad's scarf billowing behind him.

"What do I want?" Now she laughed. "What we all want. The job of our dreams, a companion for our lives, a legacy to pass onto our kids."

This time her up and down of me burned in my blood and I curled my fingers to resist the urge to adjust my robe. I would die before I showed my nerves to her. But she wasn't finished yet. "Please tell me he used a condom. The only kids I want in our marriage are the ones he puts into *me*."

There was no doubt Beth Cooper was a woman who chose her words carefully. She didn't blurt or stutter. So, I had no reason to doubt her phrasing was intended for its shock value. She intended it to hurt, but I would explode from holding it all in before I let her see she'd hit her mark.

"No worries." I pasted on a smile that would've made Katherine Hepburn jealous.

She plopped onto the sofa, crossed her Chanel boots then folded her hands. "I'm not really a horrible person."

I'd seen no evidence to support that statement. I shrugged. "I don't care what you are."

But I did. I cared so much. She was Finn's fiancée. The woman who was going to spend the rest of her life with the man of my dreams. She would carry his kids. Sleep in his bed. Be his person. And I hated her.

"Look, I know he's here, but I also know that whatever you had with him is a decade old. It's the past."

That was to imply she was his future. I smiled and didn't tell her that it didn't feel so in the past last night when he was so deep inside me, I could feel him in my heart. But I didn't think she would appreciate the crude poetry of my thoughts, so I remained silent.

"And this kind of dalliance is a one-off. He's going to be my husband. And if he cheats on me with you, I'll make sure all those videos come back to haunt his good name. I'll make sure they get yours, too."

Her tone dropped low. This wasn't an idle threat.

And I wanted to choke her. Instead, I sat down in the chair across from her. "Why are you doing this? You said yourself that you can have anyone you want."

Seriously. Wherever they lived, they'd obviously found the fountain of youth because, like him, ten years' worth of time hadn't affected her. Still blonde and beautiful, still with a smile as bright as the sun. Nary a wrinkle and if those were her real eyebrows, although they certainly didn't seem painted or enhanced, I would eat my shoe. "Why Finn?"

She might have answered had Finn not picked that moment to emerge from my room. Dressed. Dripping. Guilty. And not meeting my gaze. Not smiling. Maybe not even breathing.

"Beth." He nodded to her. "What are you doing here?"

He didn't sit beside her even though there was an entire cushion of space. He chose the other chair across from the sofa. The chair beside me with only a small table between us.

I couldn't figure out the dynamic between them. Friendship? But I didn't look at my friends the way she leered at him. But I would've bet money they weren't lovers. His scowl and stiff posture, his narrowed eye glare, and his clenched fists said lovers weren't all too likely either. It didn't really matter any more than the geography of where he sat. The only thing that mattered was the change in whatever classification they'd used to tag their relationship. The change to Mr. and Mrs., or Dr. and Mrs. because being his wife mattered. If anyone knew it, I did.

Beth smiled at him. "I came to make sure you remember your commitment to me."

Even her matter-of-fact tone grated on my nerves. But I sat silently. Hands folded. Eyes down. She turned on me anyway. "He owes me this. I couldn't get jobs because this followed me around. My name is linked to this guy."

She pointed at him without looking his way because

she was talking to me now. "To the Glouster Four. And yours wasn't. You're welcome for that, by the way."

She had to be kidding me.

"I should thank you for putting my video on national television?" She couldn't be serious. Thank her? No.

Neither was I in the mood for forgiving her or for true confession hour, but there she was like a wind-up doll who'd had her crank turned a little too hard. "I didn't mean for that to happen, and I never used your name. As soon as I could do it without it looking suspicious, I offered up a different video."

Hers. Maybe I'd misjudged her after all. When I opened my mouth to thank her for her selflessness, she waved me off. "It's not because I'm a good person, so stop looking at me like I did it to save you."

She rolled her eyes.

"I'm not a hero. I thought I'd be able to use the video of me and Finn as a steppingstone to jobs. But by the time I switched to my video, people moved on. Got tired of hearing about it."

She shrugged. "I never got another story like it."

"Did it get you better jobs?" I wasn't pointing out the flaw in her logic. I was honestly curious.

"It did for a while, that's how I got my talk show. But people don't care anymore. That's why I need him. I need my boss to know I'm no longer the silly girl he hired because I told him I had Ryder film me with Finn so I could get the story." She chuckled and shrugged like it was no big deal. "Anyway, I need Finn because I need to be married. To be settled down. I want to keep my show, and

I'm not letting whatever is going on between you two mess that up."

She swiped her hands down her legs and then stood. "So, get your shit, and let's go."

Finn pulled the corner of his lower lip between his teeth and stared at me. I looked at Beth. "We aren't divorced yet."

"Oh, right." She chuckled. "Turns out, not the problem you think it is. You'll be divorced by tomorrow. It's not a thing." She reached into her bag and pulled out an envelope. "Just need you to sign where the little tabs are."

"Have you two slept together?" I didn't know why it mattered, but I wanted to know.

Beth chuckled and shook her head. "I was saving it for the wedding night, but I was also just sitting here thinking how shameful it would be to waste this trip and the suite I booked." More of her pointed words hit their intended target, my guts.

I glanced at Finn. "Did you take money from my dad to leave me?"

He didn't answer and that said it all. I picked up the pen and signed.

One Decade Ago

Pro Tip: when embroiled in the biggest scandal experienced by a century-old college, stay away from social media, newspapers, blog posts, and anywhere else comments are welcome and can be left by users.

It wasn't really rocket science but it did speak to my desperate need to know what people were saying. The temptation to look. *Just a quick glance* would forever be the biggest lie I told myself.

But I fell so far down that hole there was no climbing back out.

Anonymous wrote, "You can't tell me this bitch didn't know she was starring on candid camera. Finn was bumping his numbers otherwise he would've never stopped dating Beth C."

And PokerPal added, "Yeah. If ever there was a step-down, he took it. And the climber could use a couple hours a week at the gym." Commentary on my freshman fifteen, the average amount of pounds gained by college freshman that I'd never bothered to lose.

In a matter of just a few keystrokes, I'd become an unattractive, fat, social climber who knew about the cameras. They commented on everything from the size of my ass to my blow job technique and the sounds I made when I was "going for a ride" versus what I sounded like when Finn was taking me to "pound town." Snippets of my video became GIFs. Boob-shots and sex faces became memes.

By the time Finn came home from wherever the hell he'd gone, my blood was boiling, my heart was broken, and my self-esteem was a fond memory I once had. I'd cried off any makeup I'd thought to put on this morning, and still, I couldn't turn away.

He glanced at me once, took a step then backtracked for another look. "What's wrong?"

His concern would've been comical, the way his face

fell, and his eyes went wide, like the bottom half of him melted while the top performed its own volcanic eruption, but this was my life. "What happened? Did somebody die?"

If that wasn't a commentary on how bad I looked, there would be no other. And instead of speaking, I twisted the laptop. I was halfway through the fifteen thousand comments, so he had a bit of scrolling to do to catch up. "Oh, shit, Lis."

He slapped the cover down over the keyboard then tossed it onto the chair and pulled me against him. "Why are you even looking at this?"

To be honest, looking hadn't started with the computer. It started with an article in the local paper, *The Maine Messenger*. The headline, "Sex Scandal Involving Chancellor's Daughter Rocks University," caught my eye, but the picture of me, an innocent ID photo, beside one of me on top of Finn's dick and next to the one of my dad kept me reading long enough to find the URL to the video, explosive reporting by the way, and type it in.

He took the paper from my lap and stared at the front page then it landed on the chair by the computer. Then he gathered me against his chest. Normally there was nowhere else I would've preferred to be, but my emotions were raw, my anger bubbling so close to the surface. I pushed him away. "You did this to me. To my dad."

Finn closed his eyes. "I know. I'm so sorry, Lis. I would give everything I have to go back and change it."

Maybe because I was hurt, because I was angry, or because some part of me really hated him for this, I pulled back, looked up at him, and lowered my voice. "And I wish I'd never met you."

I stood and walked to the bedroom. When I woke up in the morning, he was gone. And it took him ten years to come back.

13

____

Finn

She signed the papers. And I walked out. Numb. Silent.

She signed the fucking papers.

And I followed Beth to the hotel on the New Hampshire border. The drive took a couple of hours which gave me time to think about it all.

"I've made arrangements for you, Finn, because if she ever finds out what I'm about to do, I need to say I did it to help you." Chancellor Fields stood and walked around his desk. *"But you just know I'd rather see you dead than with her."*

"I'm not leaving her." My conviction, my determination was strong. Unbreakable. I thought.

"Then you don't love her. Because if you loved her, you would know this will end up destroying her. Maybe not today. Maybe not tomorrow. Maybe not until your kids use whatever technology's available in their time to look you both up and they find a

picture of their mom." He shrugged. "Maybe you'll get lucky and it won't be the one where she's sucking your dick."

There was no way to walk this back. "And if I leave her? You think that won't break her?"

Her father shook his head. "That gives her the chance to find someone else who isn't attached to the most humiliating time in her life."

What I didn't know, what I needed to find out, was too hard to ask. I cleared my throat. Then again when the lump blocking my words didn't go down. "Shit."

I covered my face with my hands, then scrubbed them up and down.

"You can start over in California. Full scholarship. Money for room and board. No student loans. You walk out a doctor and my daughter gets to forget you." He handed me an envelope. "Your plane ticket, your apartment key, some start-up cash."

I couldn't take it. Leaving her would kill me.

I held onto the notion our love would conquer all. Until I got home, and she was sitting on the sofa in a puddle of her own tears, face splotchy and swollen, eyes red, hands shaking, computer on her lap. The scandal would never die down for us if I stuck around. I did the right thing. For her. For…her.

And I signed the papers and sent them straight back, well, I did get drunk first. Toasted my soon-to-be ex-wife in a bar full of strangers who thought I was celebrating not mourning.

I didn't know she was going to burn our divorce papers up in her own drunken mournabration.

"What if my subconscious knew you'd want to get married

someday and this was my... subconscious *way of making sure I got to see you again?"*

I should've turned the car around. Marched back into that house, our house, and kissed her until she forgot I walked out on her. Again.

Fuck. *Again.* So many mistakes. No way we could come back from...all of this. Even if I could somehow manage to convince Beth to cancel the wedding, there was no way I'd ever be able to talk my way back into Felicity's life.

But I could try. I could reason with Beth. I could figure out a way to convince Felicity to give me yet another chance. And this time, I would use it well. I would make every minute of every day of her life better than the one before it.

Or I would screw it all up and we'd end up apart anyway, but at least we'd have the try we should've had before.

I pulled my car into the space next to Beth's rental and tried to calm down. I tried not to jump out and start listing my reasons why we shouldn't get married. Dealing with Beth would take finesse and patience rather than ranting and raving.

She tapped on my window. "You sleeping in the car?"

One eyebrow cocked, and a smile on her face, she pulled the door handle and leaned in. "Come on. You can pout in the comfort of our room."

She held out her hand. "And you haven't had a good pout until you've mini-bar pouted."

Only the thought of the minibar talked me out of the car. I pulled my bag from the back seat, then turned to follow her inside. In the elevator, she ran the back of her hand along the back of mine and I shifted away. There was no zing. No rush of heat. No thrill when she touched me. I'd denied myself those things for ten years, but now that I'd felt it again, I would never be able to live without them.

"Our flight leaves at two a.m." She spoke matter of factly, and I had to wonder why the hell she was bothering to tell me. She obviously would be the one making all the plans and I would be the one following blindly behind because I didn't care enough to protest. When she slipped her keycard into the slot and the light turned green, I blew out a breath.

"For fuck's sake, Finn. I'm not going to force myself on you." But in absolute contrast to her words, as soon as she walked into the room, she yanked her shirt over her head. "Besides, I think you might've had enough sex for a day?"

Probably why when she dropped her bra onto the bed, I didn't care to look. It certainly wasn't because she wasn't beautiful. Beth Cooper was as beautiful as any fashion model or actress. Blonde. Built like a Baywatch lifeguard. Being married to her and sleeping with her wouldn't be a hardship for any man who wasn't in love with the woman of his dreams. But I was and that woman wasn't Beth.

She wrapped a towel around herself and leaned her head against the doorframe to the bathroom. "That you still pine for her after all these years gives me hope."

Hope? At least one of us had some. Mine faded a little more with every minute I was away from Felicity. She closed the door, and I sighed, and listened to the water patter against the shower floor.

There were a hundred things I wanted to say to Felicity and none seemed appropriate to text, but I'd tried to call ten times. And I knew it made me creepy and stalker-like not to let it go when her not answering was a pretty clear signal, but I had to explain. One last try.

I love you, Lis. I know that it's hard for you to believe, but it's true. When I took the offer from your dad, you'd just told me that you wished you'd never met me.

No. Not her fault. Delete. Try again.

I love you. I took the money to give us both a chance to start over.

Shit. It wasn't altruistic either. Delete.

I was selfish. I thought if I took the money and went away to come back as a doctor, as someone who could give you the love you deserve, we could forget this whole thing. We could start over. You would see I was a man more than my mistakes. Without your dad's help and the money, I couldn't have done it. I'm sorry I hurt you again. I would sell my soul to change that. I'll always love you. I'll always want you. But it has to be your choice now, and sadly, the clock is ticking. I'm sorry about that, too. Please call me.

The begging at the end zapped a bit of manhood I shouldn't have been so willing to part with, but for Felicity, I would have done anything.

By the time I got the text right and hit send, Beth came out of the bathroom, dressed, smiling, hair up, makeup on.

She sat beside me on the edge of the bed. Not touching me. Not even looking at me. "She signed the papers."

Thanks for that.

"Maybe being married to me won't be so bad." Her sigh was long and deep. "Really? Finn, come on. She let you leave. She wanted you to go. I love that you still love her. It's probably the most endearing thing about you, but I *will* be a good wife."

Of course, she would. Beth Cooper didn't do anything halfway. There would be dinner on the table every night at seven. We would have the right friends. We would have kids who would be the smartest and best behaved. There'd be sex at regular intervals, enough to be satisfying, but not too much because why bother? Life with Beth Cooper wouldn't be a hardship, except for the fact I was going to love Felicity Fields for the rest of my life.

And I lost her. Not like the last time when I thought I was doing something for her, when I had a plan to come back and be the man she needed me to be. But then life happened, and I never made it back to Maine. And at some point, the dream of us faded.

Until Beth came around. Until being engaged to Beth made every minute of my day and every thought in my head filter back to Felicity.

"Beth, do you really want to be married to someone you don't love?"

She chuckled. Actually looked into my eyes and chuckled. "Where has love gotten you, Finn?"

She waved her hand in front of us. "Tell me how good you feel about love right now. You're here with me instead of with her, a her who signed the divorce papers. A her who let you walk out of her life with another woman driving the metaphorical car that was taking you away. Tell me how loving her has made your life complete."

Like the sarcastic smartass she'd always been, Beth checked her watch. When I didn't speak, she added an eye roll and dropped her wrist to her lap. "That's what I thought. Now, go shower off the ex and get gorgeous because we are going to get dinner."

I didn't feel like eating dinner. I didn't feel like doing more than climbing into bed, covering my head with a pillow to mourn the death of my relationship with Felicity. But I showered and changed because I had to play Beth's game until I could figure a way out that would not result in those videos resurfacing.

One Decade Ago

MY APARTMENT WAS every shade of blue in the color palette. Pillows, the sofa, the walls, the carpet. Whoever designed this place also has a mad love for denim. The sofa fabric, a rag rug, and the curtains all looked like someone has taken pairs of old worn jeans, sewed them together, and covered my cushions and windows. It was a lot of blue. Especially when counting the backing on the divorce papers sitting on the table.

Irreconcilable differences. Whatever the fuck that meant. Not that I didn't understand. It didn't fit was all.

I still had the money, most of it anyway, and I could pay her father back. I would lose my scholarship. Could kiss medical school goodbye. But I'd have Felicity back where she belonged. In my arms. With me. In my bed.

Or…I could finish school. I could become a doctor, pay back the money her father gave me, then go to her and show her I'm a man who had to be enough to deserve her before he came back. And if not enough, at least more than he was when he left.

Neither option gave me the warm fuzzies. So, like the best of all good decision makers, I flipped a coin. Heads: back to Maine. Tails: get the degree, then the girl.

Tails.

Then it was "two out of three." Then "three out of five." And "five out of seven." I flipped tails so many times I thought to check the very ordinary quarter to make sure it wasn't some rogue two-tailed mistake that hadn't been caught by the US Mint. Nope. Nothing radical in the coin.

It didn't stop me from flinging it at the wall, embedding it in the sheetrock.

I tried that damned coin, one like it since I couldn't get that one out of the wall, every day for a month. After class. Before class. When I awoke from a particularly wet dream about Lis. If I said heads signaled that I would go back to her, I always threw tails. If I said tails, I threw heads. Finally, I gave up.

If the universe, her dad, and an entire college chancellery didn't want us together, not to mention the woman herself who'd sent divorce paperwork, who was I to argue?

I pulled the papers off the top of the refrigerator where I'd outta-sight-outta-minded them and took a bottle of cheap vodka from the freezer then sat at the table in front of my second-hand Xbox. I was 22 and divorced. Kicked out of my choice of college. And a coin toss that didn't give a shit about my broken heart. I took two long swigs from the bottle before I could open the envelope. Another before I picked up a pen. Then with both eyes, I signed on the respondent line. Initialed each page. Signed again.

Then I curled into a ball and cried like I'd just lost my best friend.

By morning, I was ankle-deep in feelings. And hanging so far over, my chin had road rash and if I had to look into a light, my head would've exploded. And, of course, I had my Human Structure and Function class, then Clinical Skills Foundations. First, learn the body then learn how to treat it. And because I lost the girl of my dreams and the only chance I would ever have of getting her back was to become a doctor, I downed a Gatorade, stuffed my books into my bag, and left for class. Some day, I'd be able to look at Lis and not see disappointment. The alternative was unacceptable.

On the way to class, I stopped by the bank, had the papers notarized, dropped the divorce papers into a mailbox, and sent them back to Felicity. I'd let her go for now, but one day…

14

Felicity

The brisk cold air bit me as I walked, maybe stomped was more accurate, to my dad's. I rehearsed what I would say, the angry words, the accusations, I planned to hit him with. The *how could you's* and the *why's* and the *are you freaking kidding me's*.

He'd done it out of love. I knew that. Everything my dad had done in my entire life had been out of love. From the pony at my fifth birthday party to taking a job at my dream college so I would be able to get the education we both wanted me to have.

I flung his front door open as much from anger as because it was nine degrees outside and I'd just walked what felt like a thousand miles against the wind and I needed heat. I didn't just want to sit in front of his fireplace to give him hell, I needed to sit in front of the fireplace so I could warm up enough to have the discussion we needed to have.

"Dad!" Not in the kitchen, living room, office, or bedroom. Not home at all. "Shit."

I flicked on the fireplace and sat in front of it, holding my hands in front of flickering blue and orange flames. Waiting while my anger boiled just under my still freezing skin.

He'd meddled. In a way I couldn't, wouldn't forgive. Paid my husband to leave me. Which also said something about the strength of my relationship with Finn, but that was separate. An issue I couldn't focus on right now. Too hurtful. To be contemplated over a big bottle of tequila at a later date. As far out as I could manage. Maybe never because honestly, I didn't really need that kind of hangover.

When I finally warmed, when I could at least feel most of my fingers and about seventy percent of my toes, I went to the kitchen. Dad, wherever he was, would need dinner at some point and since I planned to make him drive me home after we had our conversation about Finn, dinner was the least I could do.

An hour later, chili simmering on the stove, crusty bread in the oven, and beers chilled, I turned on the TV to wait.

And like a ghost from the past, the very recent past, Beth Cooper's face filled the screen. Her perfectly arched eyebrows, clear eyes, and sunny blonde hair. Beth Freaking Cooper.

On an ordinary day, I wouldn't have watched, but Beth

Cooper hadn't done TV in Maine since she left for the west coast and became some kind of investigative reporter or some tired old shit like that. But here she was. Except this wasn't local news. This was cable news. Not just Maine. The entire nation.

And as I watched her imbibing soundlessly thanks to volume control, a picture of Glouster flashed onto the screen. A horrible sense of *oh, fuck* churned in my belly. Made my head ache. But I couldn't look away. I knew what was coming. The exact video that would play behind her as she spoke. As she brought a ten-year-old scandal back to life.

I didn't hear the door open. Didn't feel the rush of cold air as Dad stood in the doorway behind me. "Turn it off."

But I couldn't. This was my train wreck. The one I couldn't look away from. At least when the video played, they'd blacked out my face this time. But once again, my dad saw what I'd done.

For a minute, anger was difficult. A minute. Then the screen flashed to commercial, and I had a whole lot of rage needing dispensed. Starting with him.

"You paid Finn to leave me," I spoke softly because this story resurfacing wasn't going to be easy for him either. Not as a chancellor or as a father.

"I did what was right for both of you."

His arrogance wasn't anything new. I'd seen it my entire life. Usually, I found it comforting. His confidence made me feel safe. But he'd bribed my husband into ditching me.

"It wasn't your choice, Dad. You didn't have a right to…," He cocked an eyebrow, and I went silent.

"Right to protect my daughter? To give a boy who made poor choices a chance that just also happened to benefit the little girl I raised alone?" Oh, and he could do haughty and outraged better than any actress on an evening soap opera. "What did you expect me to do? Invite him to family dinner?"

As a matter of fact, yes. I did. "I expected you to let me live my life."

He laughed but not in the good way, in the condescending not a laugh at all way.

"Because you were doing such a great job?" Another scoff. "Because your TV debut was such an Oscar winner? I mean there's a proud moment, right? I got to watch my daughter…" He shook his head.

"I didn't just want him out of town. I wanted him dead. But I'm too pretty for jail."

And sarcastic. More arrogant than even two minutes ago.

He breezed past me to the kitchen where he pulled a beer from the fridge, popped it open, and took a drink before he looked over the half wall that separated the rooms.

"Felicity, you're my daughter. It's my job to make sure you have every opportunity in life. Finn Makenzie would've robbed you of any chance you might've had." He pointed the rim of his Sam Adams lager at me. "And look at you now. You're successful. Smart."

I couldn't listen to him tick off attributes that only showed half the story. I wasn't well-rounded or complete.

"I'm lonely, Dad. As in alone. Without companionship. And still on TV. Ten fucking years later." I rolled my eyes and stared as Beth Cooper's smile came back onto the big screen hanging over the fireplace. A recorded earlier tab at the top corner said this was a replay I could've lived without seeing. Without knowing existed.

How could this still be lingering? No criminal charges had ever been filed. No civil suits made. It wasn't even the anniversary. That had happened earlier in the fall. Not on the day before Christmas Eve. The day before Finn's wedding to Beth Cooper.

My heart palpitated, rejecting the thought, knowing Finn belonged with me. And I'd let him go. Again. This time, practically forced him out. I deserved this ache. Earned the sadness.

I stared at the TV. Read the caption under a picture of the university. *The scandal, ten years later, has sparked a class action suit against Glouster University.*

Oh shit.

"After the new year, a judge will decide if Glouster University can be held accountable after a decade for the videos of the victims that were posted online." And Beth Cooper elaborated while I glared at the screen.

I looked at Dad. Why hadn't he told me? "Our attorneys believe that even though they used the university's network, only the boys themselves could be held responsible and the statute of limitations against them has expired." Dad sighed. "The publicity has been bad, but I think it's going to work out. We've offered counseling for the victims, and we'll settle if we have to."

My dad was the one all my friends always thought was hot, just enough five o'clock shadow to be artsy not sloppy, dark hair, darker eyes, and no sign of a dad body. But today, I saw the lines on his face, the stress this whole situation etched into his skin. I hated that I had a part in it.

He set his empty bottle on the table next to my chair. All my life he'd been a man who didn't swear, didn't drink, didn't date. To have me as a daughter must've been quite the disappointment. Yet he'd never shown it. He'd always been there for me, and he deserved better than I'd ever been.

"Dad, I'm so sorry for..." The list would take forever. "Everything."

"All of life is a lesson. As long as you keep growing and striving to be better, there's no need to apologize." He patted my shoulder. "It's when you give up that I'll expect those I'm sorry letters and calls and skywriting."

He walked to the stove and dipped out a bowl of chili then came to sit at the coffee table. "So, he's gone?"

I nodded. Broken heart aside. "Yeah. He's getting married tomorrow."

Dad pretended not to stare at me over his spoon as he also pretended to blow it cool. "That all right with you?"

Not even a little bit. Except for the fact he'd taken money from my dad. But maybe I understood. In Glouster, he didn't have a future. He'd never have been able to become a doctor. Would have had me and nothing else if he'd stayed. And no way could I have left Glouster.

Not after everything Dad gave up for me to be able to go there.

"Yeah." But my lip quivered. And my right eye watered. Then my left. "Not really."

Dad shook his head. "What is it about that guy? You don't date. You don't go out. What hold does Finn Makenzie have on you?"

One I didn't realize. But I shrugged because no way was I shoving those words out into the ether. "I love him."

Well shit. Those words weren't better.

One Decade Ago

I STARED AT THE ENVELOPE. Stared hard enough the damned thing should've burst into flames. I wanted to ignore it, pretend it hadn't come, wish it into a disappearance Houdini couldn't undo, but there it sat, flat, mocking, on my table.

And fuck it all if I knew what to do about it. Well, the rational part of me knew what to do. Get up in the morning, take it to the courthouse, and file it. Get the divorce I now knew he wanted.

But rational me wasn't in the driver's seat. Tequila soaked me was driving this runaway train, and she had her foot hard on the pedal. And tequila me wanted to see his signature. Because if he didn't sign, we had a chance. His not taking my calls and not calling me or answering my texts didn't mean anything if he didn't sign.

I ripped open the big manilla envelope. It was just

folded brown paper with glue and a clasp. Nothing intimidating, but my fingers numbed after I touched it. I swiped them against my jeans then reached inside and pulled the papers out.

I was the petitioner. *Stupid word.* It listed Finn as the respondent. If he was here, he would have third-personed himself as *respondent* until we found something else to occupy him. Maybe even then. *Respondent would like to touch petitioner's breasts.* Or *respondent hungry,* in a deep monster voice as he chased me into the bedroom. Or *respondent loves petitioner* as he slid inside me then kissed me until nothing mattered but him.

I could hear his voice in my head. "Petitioner loves respondent, too." No one home to hear the whisper but me. I took a swig from the bottle of Cuervo for courage. I wanted and didn't want, to look at the papers.

I slid my hand into the dark inside of the envelope and felt for a loose paper because maybe he'd written me a note. But there was nothing in the envelope but the divorce papers. And I checked because if he was having second thoughts, I could work with it. I would. I wanted to. But only the papers slipped out.

I poured over every word. Not so much as a single typo or transposed number I could say ruined the validity of the papers. But because fate has always enjoyed taking her shots at me and the lawyer I'd hired was diligent to the point of perfection, the damned things were an unblemished factual representation at the end of a relationship. My relationship. And no matter how I tried, I even tried reading them in a bad British accent because nothing else worked, I couldn't distance myself from them. These were my papers with my name and the finish of my relationship.

I tossed them onto the table, picked up my bottle of tequila, and walked to flip on my iPod. I danced with only my alcohol as a partner across the same floor I'd danced with Finn a few months ago.

Hip thrusts here. A two-step there. A spin and a sashay. Until our song came on. Our fucking song. Then I folded. Every joint on my body bent so I was sitting in the middle of the floor. Drunk. Sniffling. Then sprawled and staring at the ceiling as Bon Jovi lived on a prayer then Elton John figured out why they called it the blues.

I glanced at the sofa. We'd cuddled there against the gray chenille fabric and fooled around under the cream and gray-colored throw blanket that I'd laid over the back. Then I ran my hand down the leg of the coffee table, caressing the wood where we'd sat on the floor and made a mess with ramen noodles we were trying to feed each other. Everywhere I looked, I saw him. Saw us. The great *what could've been* of my life.

It took a couple more drinks and a song so melancholy I couldn't believe I'd put it on my playlist that played. It caused my heartbreak to leak out of my eyes and down my cheeks. Another couple drinks before burning the papers sounded like a good idea.

If he wanted a divorce so bad that not even a few months of time had changed his mind, that he'd signed and returned them, then by God, he could hire his own lawyer, file his own damned papers. And I'd send them back signed with a lipstick imprint on the envelope. The bastard.

But it wasn't until I poured the papers their own shot of tequila that I could summon the courage to toss those blue-backed pages into the fireplace. Thanks to the scientific phenomenon of alcohol plus fire, the flames flared in a burst with a sizzle then wisps of smoke floated up the chimney, along with the last traces of my happiness.

I went into my room and cried myself to sleep.

15

Finn

Beth Cooper didn't snore. Or leave her clothes on the floor. Or sing in the shower. Or do one endearing thing that made me think the lifetime I was about to promise to spend with her would be anything more than desolate. Desperate. Without a single quirk or charming idiosyncrasy.

No surprises. No foibles that led to long nights of talking or making out under store awnings or holding hands while we took turns stirring spaghetti sauce. We wouldn't kiss in the rain. There would be no spontaneous acts of love that reminded me of how lucky I was.

Regret curled my shoulders as I sat in the aisle seat next to Beth on the plane. Two hours into a six-hour flight, I flipped on the screen embedded into the back of the seat in front of me. Thank fuck for technology. I could watch the Christmas edition of Sports Center or a replay of whatever game was on. I flipped through the screens, giving each one a couple seconds of play time before moving on. And then it happened.

I didn't have the earphones plugged in yet, so it took a few seconds for me to realize what I was seeing. A few more for my brain to decipher what it meant. And three after that for me to turn to Beth.

Her eyes were wide. Her lined in pink mouth hanging open. Then, while I watched, her skin flushed to the darkest, deepest red I'd ever seen.

"What. The. Fuck?" Her voice was steel, deadly, deep. And I concentrated on that. On the fact that I was sitting on a plane next to the woman who swore if I married her this story would die with her. Turned out we were both liars. And neither of us very good at it.

I read the ticker at the bottom of the screen. *Class action.* The words blurred and I refocused on a foursome of pictures that flashed onto the screen above each of our names. *Ryder Kennedy. Jameson King. Keaton Shaw. Finn Makenzie.* And Beth's *what the fuck* wasn't so far off the mark. But when a picture of the hospital where I worked flashed onto the screen, my stomach rolled, and I flicked the power button to off.

Oh, God.

While I mourned the life I'd had, nothing more glaring than the first squandered chance with Lis and now a second, and the one I'd hoped to return to as a well-respected ER doctor, Beth checked social media. Every couple seconds, or every few slides of her finger, she swore a little louder, a little stronger, and a little angrier.

She turned to me and held up the screen.

"That bitch!" She unfastened her seat belt. "That's my story. My fucking show." And Beth finally had her moment, the one where maybe fate or karma or the big guy upstairs had stepped in to show all of us that there were consequences to lies and blackmail. And whatever the force doing the throwing was, it got both of us with one stone.

"If she thinks for one second I'm going to let her steal my show, my seat on that stage, she's as stupid as she is fake." She twisted the screen toward me again so I could see the woman who'd been telling the Glouster scandal story. Blonde. Bright smile. Business suit uniform. Could've been Beth's sister had their parents been brave enough to make two of them. The loud one next to me growled, then slapped the top of my thigh with her knuckles.

"Fake!" She punched a finger into the screen and continued ranting so that the lady across the aisle stared at us. "Honestly. This bitch has enough bought and paid for parts to build a whole new woman. Look at her!"

No way was I dumb enough to remind Beth she too had her fair share of silicone and Botox. But she narrowed her eyes at me anyway. "Just shut up."

And the next four hours followed a similar pattern until we had an audience, plenty of support for the wronged Beth Cooper, and a couple old ladies staring at me as if Beth showing them some ten-year-old footage meant I couldn't have grown, couldn't have repented.

By the time we taxied to the terminal, the other passengers had whipped Beth into an angry hate-spewing rage machine who didn't wait for the plane to stop rolling before she called her boss, Maxwell something or other.

"You...son of a bitch...I saw Rachel Novak..." As her voice rose, cheers erupted from the aisle where everyone else was lined up to deplane. "That's...right...really?" Her voice changed. Dropped a few octaves and her eyes narrowed. Then came the smile. A slow slide of happiness that transformed her entire face. "Really?"

Her fingers dug into my biceps. "Oh my God, thank you so much!"

She hung up her cell and kissed me hard then looked at the passengers watching us.

"I'm not losing my show." But she glanced at me and frowned. "We have to talk."

"Okay." But we were twelve hours from our sunset wedding, and I needed a nap, but we still had to find our way off the plane, navigate through the airport, and to our respective apartments to get ready before heading to the venue. There would be plenty of time to talk later. And since she already had her promotion, she'd at least be in a good mood when we had this big conversation. When I stood, she pulled me down beside her. Because she always meant now. Something I would have to get used to. Time waited for no woman, and Beth Cooper refused to waste a second of it.

"Oh, you mean now." Fine. This was my opportunity. At the same time, I said, "I'm not marrying you," she said, "I'm not marrying you."

"What?"

I'd spent six months listening to details about sequins versus rhinestones, lilies versus roses, photographs versus video. Not to mention the entire day I spent at a spa before we could get our engagement pictures taken, the thousands of dollars in new clothes and the car she'd insisted I buy, appearances were everything, didn't I know, and I'd walked out on Felicity again. This time she'd told me to, but I hadn't fought, hadn't hung around to convince her, Felicity, she couldn't live without me.

She rolled her eyes. "Don't pretend like you're not peeing your pants right now you're so happy. We both know I can't marry you for several reasons."

And because of all the things I did know, when to quit wasn't one of them, I sat back and stared. "That's fair. Because I can't marry you either. I love her, Beth, and you deserve someone who wants to be with you like I want to be with her."

She pulled her head back and chuckled like I'd just told her she couldn't stick a fork into a light socket at the same moment she stuck a fork into the light socket. "Thank God. Because the Glouster scandal and the class action suit is bound to come biting at your ass any minute now. And I can't very well be the sympathetic victim if I'm married to one of the named perpetrators, now can I?"

As far as points went, this one made sense. "Pardon me, but that isn't what I want to be remembered for. And it's not the way I want to be introduced career-wise." Wasn't that her big threat a couple weeks ago when I agreed to be her husband? "But mostly, I can't marry you because for as good a kisser as you are, I do not want to spend the rest of my life getting half-assed kissed by a guy who wants someone else."

"I haven't half-assed kissed anyone in my entire life." Important to me that she knew it, too. Not that I wanted to kiss anyone but Felicity, but my pride couldn't take too many more hits.

Her responding chuckle didn't enhance my ego at all, either.

"In that case, maybe the memory of kissing you is better than actually kissing you." She shrugged. "Anyway, we're at the airport, and we both know that there's nowhere else you'd rather be than letting the little wife untie your bow for Christmas. So, go. Or don't go and be miserable for the rest of your life. But now it's on you. Not me."

She reached into her bag and pulled out the divorce papers she had in her hand.

I smiled because for the first time in ten long years, I could see the possibility of a light, a happiness. "It would have been so much better if we'd figured this out about six hours ago."

But I kissed her cheek. I'd been given my fair share of chances in life. Seconds. Thirds. Some I'd wasted. Some I'd made the most of. But none was ever so important to me as this one. And no way in hell was I going to let it pass me by.

16

Felicity

Christmas in Glouster was straight out of one of those romantic movies with carolers and warm, mulled cider, carriage rides, stores aglow with lights and sparkling ornaments made of glitter and glass that made this whole place look like Santa was a year-round resident. We had a live nativity, a nightly reenactment of the twelve days of Christmas as sung and acted by members of each class at the elementary school. The librarian, Mrs. O'Toole, sat in a heated tent and read "The Night Before Christmas" on Monday, Wednesday and Friday, then directed the Glouster players in an abridged version of *A Christmas Carole.* If there was a holiday tradition Glouster missed, I could never imagine what it was.

And we handed out gifts to all the kids, snapped photos with our Santa, we had two, one modern, one a vintage version with a long robe and holly berries twined around his head like a Christmas wreath. Old fashioned Santa, Marty, my lawyer, was normally more popular with the older folks, and yeah, they all still posed for photos with him, but this year, some of the younger families were in line for him, too.

We sold the cider, sang the carols, with ho-ho-hos abounding along with cheek kisses, wishes for a Merry Christmas and a Happy New Year, and visions of the requisite sugar plum, blah blah blah. Glouster took its celebrations seriously.

And tonight, because I'd avoided it all week in favor of spending time with Finn, it was my turn to man the Santa hut and the Polaroid camera while I wrangled kids on and off Modern Santa's lap and handed out candy canes to the tiny tots who, for this one night of the year, couldn't wait to get home to bed so they could get up in the morning and open their gifts.

At least it kept me away from the cider stand and Sofia who was selling two shots of vodka for every cup of cider she handed across the counter to whichever mom or dad was in charge of beverages.

In the Snapshots with Santa hut, we'd whittled the line of kids down to none, so Santa and I took a break. He headed for the bathroom in the hardware store, and I walked to the cider stand.

"Hand me one of those." I nodded to the steaming mug with the quaint hand-drawn picture of a hometown Glouster Christmas glazed into the side.

She held up an airline-sized bottle of Smirnoff. "You want some lead in it?"

The last thing I needed was alcohol to enhance or adversely influence the emotions I could barely keep at bay now. In the happiest place on the east coast. On Christmas Eve. "Nah. This is fine."

She shrugged and pocketed the vodka. "He left?"

I nodded then held out my hand. Instead of pouring the vodka into my drink, I gripped it and stared. It was going to take a lot more than this tiny thing to stop the breaking of my heart. I shoved it into the bell-bedazzled pocket of my elf suit.

"Bastard."

"It's fine." Really.

It was.

Not.

Fine at all. Nothing was fine.

But since there wasn't anything I could do short of calling him, begging him to come back to me, forgiving him for lying to me, I already had but he was going to have to work for it before I ever said the words, forgiving myself for driving him away.

The arrogance to think I would get or that I deserved a second chance was something hardwired into my DNA, but I knew he wouldn't come back now. He'd done it already and I sent him away. Besides, any minute, he was about to pledge his life, and probably his soul, to Beth. Even if they couldn't make it official until the day after Christmas.

"What time are you off tonight?"

She always came to Dad's with me for Christmas Eve. We ate and watched *It's a Wonderful Life* then we went to bed. In the morning we opened the gift cards Dad always bought for us for book stores and spa treatments and he opened the new ties, shirts, and whatever classic book we managed to find for him. This year I'd found a first edition Dickens. Last year, a Bronte. He loved all the classics. But Sofia was going to be with Dakota this year. Tomorrow, they would celebrate with me and Dad. Everything was changing.

"Seven." She cleared her throat. "You know, you could fly out there and stand up when the preacher asks if anyone objects."

I chuckled. Because I'd considered it. "The wedding was this afternoon. I think."

Or maybe it was this evening. But this evening California time. Which was practically the middle of the night my time. The moment I decided not to do the math to see if I could make it before the I do's were done was the moment I gave up on even the hope of me and Finn being anything more than history.

Sofia shook her head, and I could've sworn her eyes went dark with disappointment. "You're such a quitter."

"I'm not a quitter. Our ship sailed. We forgot to board. It happens. Now he's marrying someone else. And I'm going to move on." The words felt big. The idea bigger, but the truth was nothing more than a sliver of it. Because at that moment, all I wanted to do was spend the rest of my life remembering the eleven best days of my youth and the week I got to spend with him as an adult. But I didn't want pity or blind dates or third-wheel dinners.

And so, the lie became necessary. And we both knew it.

"Any prospects on the horizon?" Her voice had just enough hope in it to make me feel pathetic and more than a little defensive because no, there were no prospects on the horizon. There never were. Chances were, there never would be either. But I couldn't tell her that without enticing the blind date brigade into action.

She smiled at me, and I cleared my throat. It was as if she was daring me to tell my fib.

"Well, no." And I just wasn't up to it. "He just left today. Wasn't a lot of time to swipe right."

"Yeah." She nodded. "So, you'll be moping for…a couple months before I should rally the single guys in town?"

She grinned, but she was serious. This wasn't a new road, and she'd helped me survive it last time. And because she was a real friend, who'd seen me through all the big heartaches in my life, she didn't sugarcoat anything. She knew me. "Or do you plan to go full-on old maid now?"

"I told him to go." And regrets did no good. Although I had them aplenty, and as someone who knew me so well, she cocked an eyebrow. "Fine. Give me a month, tops. Then I'll find a guy and go on a date. We'll get married. Have kids. You can be Auntie Sofia. We'll get a dog. Just let me have a month of peace."

We lived in a college town. People rotated in and out. Of course, most of them were a lot younger than me now. But maybe Dad knew a nice, kind of cool, hipster professor I could see. This time, I would give it a fair try. Maybe something good would come of it. Or maybe I'd end up the crazy cat lady.

I was happy Sofia had Dakota. That they were so in love

made me, not jealous, but happy for them, and I understood that she wanted everyone to feel the same joy she felt, but I needed some wallowing time. A few days to cry it out, then a few more to pull it together, then a few weeks to get some direction, and spruce myself up so I didn't send any prospective date running for cover.

Most of the townies, the common moniker the non-college students who lived in Glouster shared, were out enjoying the festivities. Mr. and Mrs. Duncan along with their brood of four toddlers from ages one to four were waiting for a carriage ride. The Danes sisters, Ora and Olla, were handing out candy canes to everyone they passed, and I had to wonder how deep Ora's purse went because her entire arm disappeared inside for every piece of candy she went in after. Captain Jack, local police, was manning the reindeer petting station. For a second, I considered him. He was in his late thirties with a smattering of gray strands of hair mixed in with the coal black at his temples, his face was angular and chiseled. Handsome. And single. If ever I moved past my broken heart, maybe…

Then there was Coren Lee, the pride of Glouster. She had a singing show on local cable that aired every Sunday morning and featured her singing and dancing to the latest Top Forty hits. Probably violated about a hundred copyright laws or whatever covered music rights, but she was so cute and so bubbly no one dared mention things as trivial as the law.

This town was full of people I'd come to love and care about. People who'd taken me in and let me be a part of something. No way could I leave here, and Finn had a life in California he'd built for himself. Maybe it was better to leave everything as it was, fond memories of a time when life was simpler and more complicated.

And speaking of people I loved, an arm slipped around my shoulder as Dad leaned in. "Merry Christmas, sweetheart."

I smiled then quirked a brow. Dad hadn't walked up to me alone. He was with Professor Masterson. Leah Masterson. I knew her vaguely. Too vaguely for her to look up at my dad with one arm around his waist and one laid on his chest. We were in public for goodness sake.

"Fliss, you know Professor Masterson."

She held out her hand. "Please, call me Leah."

Ah right, Professor Masterson. I nodded, on the wrong side of stunned. "Yeah. Good to see you again."

She'd been my English professor. I cocked a brow at Dad and saw the smile, the slight strain of color on his cheeks, the body language tilting toward her. After thirty years without a woman other than a daughter in his life, my dad had a girlfriend. And a good daughter would've been happy for them.

I was not such a daughter. "So…"

I nodded to Leah. My question, *should I call her Mommy*, communicated through a stare. His reply, *time will tell, and I hope so*, came back with a smile.

Dad chuckled. "We'll see you girls tonight?"

Sofia, who'd previously decided to spend this evening with her man, nodded like an uncontrollable bobblehead doll. "You bet. We're so there."

"Good. See you tonight." He winked. My. Dad. Winked. Then he walked away, with a woman, like it was as natural as his breathing. But my mom ran off just after I was born, and I had never seen my dad so much as smile at another woman. There was nothing normal about him being with a woman.

And we would've had a discussion about it, because I *needed* to discuss it, needed to hear myself say how happy I was for him, to try it out and make sure it was true. Because if anyone deserved happiness, it was my dad. And I didn't want to ruin this for him, so if I couldn't honestly be happy, and I wasn't sure if I could or couldn't, I at least needed Sofia to help me figure out how to fake it.

But Sofia's phone buzzed and she frowned at the screen, then turned away to answer. "Hello?" She spoke with quiet tentativeness so foreign to her naturally bubbly self, I chuckled. "Um, yes. But…I'm at the festival…"

She paused, looked at me, then drew her gaze away. She'd gone from nervous to downright shifty. "Yes…until 7 pm…"

There was something strange going on, but the line at the Santa hut had grown, and I had to get back. I waved and left her to her conversation. Talking about Dad would just have to wait, or I would have to figure out how to deal with it myself. Which I would because Dad deserved the same support he'd always given me.

Decision made, I walked back to the hut. Then it was three more hours of ho-ho-hos, peppermint candy, and wish lists that contained everything from Play-doh to hoverboards and all the little do-dads and what-nots in between.

Finally, 7 o'clock rolled around, and it was time to close up. The crowd had dwindled to almost nothing, and I picked up my bag from behind Santa's chair.

I could feel his gaze. "Great job tonight, Santa."

It was really Randy Allen. He'd been Santa every year since I was in college. Kids loved him and he fit the suit.

"You, too." And not for the first time, he sounded like Finn. Sometimes it happened that way for me. I would see him in places he couldn't possibly be, hear him when there was no chance it could be him. I'd gotten used to it. Too used to it.

17

Finn

God, she was beautiful. Even in her crazy green knitted dress lined with fur at the neck and hem, her black boots with the low-heels also lined with fur, and the hat with bells that jingled every time she moved and little pieces of plastic on each side that fit over her ears and made them pointed. And she smelled like heaven, flowery and clean in a room meant to smell like Christmas with its pine candle and hidden Christmas tree air fresheners. And oh God, the smile, genuine and sweet, no matter who she aimed it at. All of it, all of her, made sitting in this awful chair pretending to be from the North Pole while what felt like every kid in town climbed on my lap all worth it.

Felicity pulled her purse from behind my chair, and I caught a big whiff of her. Sunshine. And flowers. Something that would always be just her.

I'd forgotten too many things about her and not nearly enough. She had eyes brighter than the sun, more expressive than a painting. Her laugh was like music and made my heart lighter. These were the things I assumed everyone knew about her.

But I'd not remembered the way her voice went husky with just a slight rasp when she wanted me. And the way she could be so intense when she cooked. Her touch was like a hundred feathers on my skin and I'd always loved the way her face lit up when she petted a dog or talked about the cat, De Luna, she'd had before they moved to Glouster. How had I forgotten those things?

She smiled over her shoulder. "Great job tonight, Santa."

"You, too." She stopped for just a second and moved as if she was going to turn to look at me. Fuck. I'd blown my cover and Sofia didn't have time to set everything up yet. But then Lis started rooting through her bag again, and I breathed out slow. Soft. It took every ounce of will I had not to stand, wrap my arms around her and pull her back into me. To close my eyes and hold her.

She found her keys and jingled them in her hand. "I should go."

And that was it. The thought of her walking away, even though I knew where I'd find her, made me stand, and move between her and the small door. "Lis."

She glanced up at me. Looked down. Scoffed and shook her head. Even over the candle that was supposed to smell like a Douglas fir, I could smell her shampoo, the lotion that matched, and the hand sanitizer that all came from one of those mall stores where she could mix her own fragrances. A smell that would always belong to her.

A smell that made my voice small, cracked. I smiled. If she told me to leave I was going to die, and I always wanted to go out with a smile on my face. Even if it was fake as hell. "Surprise."

She narrowed her eyes, not quite a glare, but nowhere near a look of joy. "You've been here all this time?"

I wasn't sure whether to duck or hug her. So, I didn't move at all. Partly because I only had this one chance to make this right and *not* lose her a third time. Partly because she was stunning and sometimes staring at her made it impossible for me to do anything else. This was one of those minutes.

She cleared her throat, set her bag on the table, and crossed her arms. "What are you doing here?"

It was my chance to say something clever and romantic, something that would express everything I felt for her so there were no blurred lines or confusion about us. "I love you."

And while that summed it up, no way was it enough. "I didn't marry Beth."

Not even close to what I wanted to say, but definitely something she needed to know. Maybe it was jetlag. I'd been up all night and spent so much time on planes today. An excuse for my lack of finesse.

"Oh. Good."

I opened the front of my Santa suit and pulled out the envelope of papers Beth had handed me at the airport. "And we're not divorced."

Those words made my heart flex its muscle.

"How did you get here?"

In here?

"In this little cottage? I had some help from Sofia." I shrugged. "When your real Santa went to the bathroom, she cornered him and waited for me to show up so I could put on the suit."

But if she meant in Maine, that was a little more complicated. Something we could discuss after I kissed her. After I gave her the ring I'd been hanging onto for the last ten years.

I didn't have a fancy box or even a little velvet pouch. It was loose in my pocket and I reached in and pulled it out. "Lis…"

I moved closer, and she didn't step back, so I took it as a good sign. "I love you. I always have, and this last week has been…amazing. I can't go back to being without you, Lis. I can't let you go again."

Her hand was warm and soft, and she didn't use it to punch me as I held it in mine and lifted the ring to slip over her knuckle.

Tears welled in her eyes. Her mouth formed a tiny little O. Her fingers squeezed mine. This was so much more than I deserved. To be in her life at all was always over the top but to see her wearing the ring I'd bought a lifetime ago… hers weren't the only cheeks with tears rolling down them. "If you let me, I'm going to spend the rest of my life loving you."

I stepped closer, angled our bodies, and held her. "I will wake you up every morning and put you to bed every night with a kiss, and I'll make sure every day you know you're loved and cherished." She blinked a few times and sniffed. I was getting to her. "And I'm going to make up every day we were apart. Because there's no one in my life more important than you are."

I swallowed hard. The words were easy, speaking was not because of my heart sitting so squarely in my throat. "I love you and your heart and your soul, and that when no one else loved me or thought I could be something, you did. You believed in me."

She nodded. "You're easy to believe in."

A tear slipped down her cheek and I caught it on the pad of my thumb and wiped it away.

"I want to spend the rest of my life with you. Holding you. Kissing you. Talking to you. Loving you."

"Me too." She smiled and leaned her forehead against my chest. "I mean I want that, too."

But I had to tell her the truth, what we were going to go through. "Lis…"

"Tomorrow we can talk about the lawsuit, but tonight's our first Christmas Eve." She tangled her fingers in my hair, used her free hand to yank the fake beard down, then lifted her chin and pressed her mouth against mine.

Our first Christmas Eve. One of hopefully many.

EPILOGUE

Finn

"Paging Dr. freaking Makenzie!" There was a certain urgency to her voice. A tone that compelled me to move quickly toward the bed. My yellow paper apron crinkled and bunched, but my wife needed me. And by God, a rumpled mess or not, I was there.

Of course, I wasn't in the room in an official capacity, not more than as the guy who loved his wife and needed to be with her as she brought our baby into the world. I'd lobbied for physician's rights, but Lis vetoed the idea without much listening to my arguments. Something about it being weird for me to deliver the baby, my baby, who would be delivered by her OB-GYN. Honestly, I was too nervous to be a good doctor for either of them.

Also trembling. And proud. An odd mix of emotions.

I slipped my fingers through hers. "I'm here, Lis."

I remained calm, channeling my inner zen. Or something else ridiculous our Lamaze coach had preached.

Felicity shot me a half glower. "Maybe next time you can have your legs in the stirrups, and I'll go out into the hall and flirt with the nurses."

I kissed her forehead. "Sweetheart, you're the only woman in the world I want to flirt with."

She did a couple of he-he-he patterns of breathing then vise gripped my hand while the doctor worked under the blanket draped over Lis's knees.

"Big push, Felicity." She looked up at me, glared, then closed her eyes, grunted, and squeezed my hand. In pain. Beautiful. Brave. So much more than I deserved.

In the last nine months, we'd moved into a bigger house, decorated a baby's room, celebrated her dad's wedding, and prepared to become parents. Turned out that the one time we hadn't used a condom during that magical week of being back together, we'd created a life. One currently fighting its way to the outside world.

And as wonderful as things had turned out, they weren't perfect. As I suspected, Ryder, Jameson, Keaton, and I were all named in the lawsuit that started against the school and widened its scope to include us as defendants. The videos were back on TV, the scandal as fresh as it was a decade ago. And now there were lawyers and depositions, witness subpoenas, testimony preparation, and my wife had stood beside me through it all. Damn, I loved her.

She choked my hand again and I stared down at her. "You're doing great."

Because it was what I was supposed to say. But she

widened her eyes and panted at me. "Just think, no more swollen ankles."

"Yeah." She nodded and breathed in through her nose. "More. Tell me more."

"Oh. Shit. Um…you won't pee every time you sneeze." I brushed her hair off her forehead then patted it dry with a washcloth.

"Thanks for bringing that one up." But she smiled a little. "What else?"

"No more back cramps. Or puking when you smell broccoli." She'd had a rough time since the only food she craved, constantly, was the one that made her stomach rebel. "Or needing help to get out of bed."

The doctor peeked at her over the cover. "On the next contraction, push again. Hard. With everything you got left."

I kissed Felicity because I'd never seen such courage, such determination. Plus, I wanted her to know I was there. Wanted her to know if she needed me, I would do whatever I could do to help her.

"Tell me more, Finn." She squeezed her eyes closed and clenched my hand as she grunted out another push.

"You'll be able to tie your own shoes. Hell, you'll be able to see those cute little feet. And we'll both fit in the shower again." The shower in the new house was half the size of the one in our cottage by the college. And once she got further along into the pregnancy, it was too tight a squeeze for us to shower together, and more than once she'd cried over it. Full-on, sobbed.

"Yes!" And then I heard it. The first cry. Tinny. Small.

But full of life. Angry to be thrust into the light, but then quiet as the nurse laid our baby girl across Lis's chest and they both cooed.

"Oh, my God." She squeezed my hand, softer this time, but as powerful as before when coupled with her tears of happiness and her smile. "Look at her, Finn."

Like I could take my eyes off such a beautiful baby. She had Felicity's full, red lips, her chin, and even her long, dainty fingers. And now my life was complete. There were two of them, two women in my life I would die to make happy, two people I would always love more every day for as long as I lived.

"My family." And despite the details that continued to leak out in the press about the upcoming trial and the media coverage that seemed to get more intense every day, enough so, there was already a story about Felicity, victim and current wife of one of the Glouster Four, being in labor, I would, now and forever, make sure my wife and daughter knew how much I loved them.

~ A billionaire revenge romance series ~
Twisted Beauty
Twisted Love
Twisted Fate

Mafia's Obsession
~ A hot mafia romance series ~
Mafia's Dirty Secret
Mafia's Fake Bride
Mafia's Final Play

Screaming Demons
~ An MC romance series full of suspense ~
Rough Start
Rough Ride
Rough Choice
Rough Patch
Rough Return
Rough Road
Rough Trip
Rough Night
Rough Love

Standalone Contemporary Romance
Billionaire in Vegas
Billionaire Hunt
Billionaire's Game
Billionaire Retreat
Billionaire On Air

A Chance To Love
Somebody To Love
Not Mine To Love

141

Check out Summer's entire collection at
www.summercooper.com/books

www.ingramcontent.com/pod-product-compliance
Lightning Source LLC
Chambersburg PA
CBHW031237210726
48287CB00003B/803